Mussolini's Hat

KATHLEEN JONES

The Book Mill

Acknowledgements

This is a work of the imagination. All
the characters are fictional and bear no
resemblance to anyone living or dead.
Any similarities are entirely accidental.

My thanks to Alexander Kleinloh
for the kind permission to use one of
his Acquerelli for the cover design.

In Memoriam

Medea Saporetti and Marco Marini

. .At times it returns,
in the motionless calm of the day, that memory
of living immersed, absorbed, in the stunned light.'

Cesare Pavese, *The Night*

Contents

Twelve stories

Twelve people

One small Italian town

The People

Babacar	A Senegalese street trader.
Anastasia Segreto	Half Georgian, half Calabrian. Widow, owner of Fidel.
Carla Falcone	Gallerista.
Franco Moretti	Owner of the Pizzeria del Duomo.
Stefania Moretti	Franco's wife.
Martin Soulby	English Sculptor.
Pia Konstantinou	Greek barista at the Bar di Pietro.
Matteo	Pia's boyfriend, son of Enzo, owner of the Bar di Pietro.
Enzo	Property owner, Fascist, divorced.
Eva	Barista at the Bar di Pietro, mistress of Enzo.
Mari-Elena	Divorced wife of Enzo, mother of Matteo, living in Torino.
Clara	The midwife, widow of Tommaso. Known as 'Nonna'.
Father Hermes	A Franciscan Friar, from Lebanon.
Simona	Single parent, mother of Paolo.

11

Vittorio	The old man Simona cleans for.
Angelina Gallo	The old woman who takes Simona's place.
Avvocato Baldacchini	The lawyer.
Marina and Olimpia	The two sisters who run the shoe shop.
Rosa	Widow who has a shop selling fresh pasta.
Giorgio and Luca	Two elderly brothers, formerly artigiani working in the studios.
David	English violinist who busks in the piazza.
Taj	Tibetan Italian who busks in the piazza.
Rose Umber	Canadian sculptor in Italy on a scholarship.
Pierluigi	Very attractive artigiano in the Studio Bertolozzi.
Shira	Israeli. Owns Studio Bertolozzi.
Frida and Carl	Two Swiss tourists.
The Beautiful Girls	Angelina, Mariella, Elena, Catalina
The Albanian Boys	Nico, Arjan, Leo, Rezar, Zamir

The Town

This is Italy. The twentieth century is dead and the new millennium has already forgotten its first decade and is rolling relentlessly through the second. It all feels peculiarly modern, but around you are buildings, objects, vistas that have been settled in their places for thousands of years. Our little *Citta d'Arte* for instance. The history of it goes back so far it is almost its own museum. The walls of the town are made from stone blocks laid so tightly against each other you can barely put a blade of grass in the cracks – the kind of masonry that the Greeks and Etruscans knew how to construct, named for a one-eyed god. The gateway, the Porta dei Medici, is a later feature with marble columns eroded by weather and an imposing archway that is rumoured (falsely) to have been designed by Michelangelo.

He lived here once, working for the Medici, sourcing the pure, almost translucent, white marble they call *statuario* – carving wonders such as the 'David' that stands in the Uffizi gallery in Florence. But Michelangelo Buonarroti wasn't a happy man. His letters to his employers are in the old library behind the Duomo. Apparently he found his lodgings inferior, the pay inadequate and he complained regularly about both the weather and the wine. Apart from the weather, things have improved since then.

For maximum impact, it's best to enter the town by the western gate, the one facing the sea. When the Etruscans lived here, the sea lapped almost to the pavement on the other side of the road, but it has since retreated, the old moorings have silted up, and the beach

13

is now almost a mile away across a flat strip of cultivated ground, criss-crossed by irrigation canals and decorated with horticultural poly-tunnels that reflect the light like mirrors.

When you walk through the Porta dei Medici the piazza opens out in front of you with a theatrical flourish, and the first thing you notice is the Duomo, flashing white marble in the early light, its steps glossy with overnight rain. Behind the Duomo, beyond the walls of the town, the marble mountains are shaking themselves out of the clouds. You glimpse shoulders of grey granite, seams of white marble that might even be snow, and the sheer faces of forbidding crags, scoured by scree. Lower down, the slopes are covered in pine forest, then sweet chestnut trees, olive groves and vineyards. The salty Mediterranean winds give a unique character to the local wine.

The town is caught between these two ways of living – its back to the mountains; its face to the sea. The weekly market in the piazza is full of local produce that reflects this landscape – cheese, olives, chestnuts, chickens, eggs, oranges, persimmon, peaches, salted fish, anchovies and sardines, wild boar sausages and salami and bottles of local wine, both red and white. There are courgettes, green chard and tomatoes from the polytunnels, and potatoes from the fertile silt of the plain.

Inside the old walls the streets are arranged geometrically with Roman precision – three main thoroughfares leading off the piazza to the north and south, intersected by smaller lanes that are so narrow the buildings almost touch. There is a northern gate opening onto a car park, and a southern gate, the Porta da Pisa, that gives access to a new housing estate, but to the east only the formidable bulk of La Rocca – the only remnant of a fortification dating back to the Etruscans – straddles the rocky incline where the mountains form an impregnable barrier. From La Rocca you have an almost aerial view of the town, and can see out over the Mediterranean where the spine of Corsica interrupts the watery horizon in a blue haze.

Behind the Duomo, on one of the side streets, is the old Abbey of St Francis, with its crumbling cloisters and a long monastic building that extends almost the length of the street, though the windows are shuttered and only half a dozen Franciscan monks remain. Only two of them are Italian, the rest are recruits from South America or the Levant. The monastery is dying, unlike the cafés, restaurants and bars that proliferate around the piazza and the streets that run from it. There are designer fashion shops and art galleries and enotecas heaving with Americans and Germans and Japanese – for this is the *Citta d'Arte*, where Michelangelo lived and worked, visited by Giordano Bruno and Dante. It has attracted sculptors, painters and poets for more than a thousand years.

But at this time in the morning it's quiet. In the dawn light the partly-raised shutters of the apartments look like half-open eyelids. The rectangular expanse of marble paving that is the piazza is as empty as a chequered gaming board waiting for the pieces to be taken out of the box.

At the far end, below the steps leading to La Rocca, is the obligatory statue of Vittorio Emmanuele, and beside him an animal perched on top of a tall column – presumed to be the emblem of the town. Its identity has long since been eroded into anonymity. A lion? There is certainly the remnants of a mane, but there is also the stump of what could have been a wing. Perhaps a griffin? No one knows.

Today there is also some scaffolding and a wooden stage bolted together in anticipation of the evening celebrations of *'Capo d'Anno'*. The Michelangelo tower is already wired with fireworks. New Year's Eve is taken very seriously here.

At six o'clock the bells in the campanile begin to tumble and chime, to wake anyone still asleep. Some of the boutique lights are on and there is a light in the upstairs window of the elderly shoe sisters, Olimpia and Marina. They are early risers. None of the marble studios are awake yet. The bar on the corner has unlocked its door, anticipating the first customers, but there is no sign of Matteo or his girlfriend Pia. No one is stirring at the Pizzeria del Duomo on the opposite corner either, but that's not unusual. Franco shuts late and opens late, the hour depending on the size of last night's hangover.

In an apartment on Via Giordano, Anastasia Segreto is fast asleep with her old dog, Fidel, over her feet. She has been awake half the night, worrying about her financial situation. At the Misericordia the Tibetan busker, Taj, is folding his sleeping bag, and down on the waste land of an abandoned marble yard the young Albanian refugees are emerging from their peculiar assortment of old caravans – some without wheels, propped up on marble blocks left behind when the yard closed. The Albanian boys don't seem to mind. They're smoking cigarettes and one of them is lighting a fire in a discarded oil drum to boil a kettle.

Clara, the old midwife, who lives above the café, is already drinking her first coffee, propping her elbow on the window sill to look down over the piazza. A rather battered Apè is trundling through, with the insignia of the *comune* on the side. A man is throwing bags of rubbish into the trailer, picking up dropped ice cream cups and cigarette ends with a long stick.

Rosa is outside her pasta shop, swilling the pavement with soapy water. She has some focaccia dough proving in the kitchen and by 7am there will be brioche too, oozing with custard. A ragout is bubbling on the stove, sauce for the ravioli she will make later when the filling cools. She is one of the last of the old trades to have a foothold in the piazza. Her family own the building but she knows that when she dies her children will sell it for expensive apartments and her pasta shop will become a boutique, or a restaurant, like all the others.

The strengthening light is reading the history of the landscape. The marble mountains first, then the Michelangelo tower, the walls of La Rocca, then the cupola of the Duomo, and last of all the grandiose Napoleonic apartment blocks that line the piazza.

Suddenly the clouds that shroud the mountains seem to spring apart and the winter sun shoulders its way out into the open sky. Everything looks curiously naked, as if reluctant to be looked at, caught unawares *in flagrante delicto*. This is the last day of the old year. No one has any idea what is going to happen in the new.

1

Mussolini's Hat

The bell tolling from the campanile wakes Pia from an uneasy, late siesta. There's a stillness in the room, perhaps an illusion created by the dark winter evening and the sound of the rain falling outside, muffling every sound but Matteo's breathing and the distant pealing of the bell. She wonders what time it is; whether she has overslept. Matteo is dreaming, one arm flung across the pillow, his mouth open. He looks childlike and vulnerable. Pia's skin is still sticky with sex as she slides out from under the quilt. She looks at her mobile on the bedside table. It's just after 9pm. Time for a quick shower before she goes down to the bar.

She can hear Eva moving glasses around downstairs. Beyond the window, the rain is falling as it has been all afternoon. Not a light Mediterranean shower, but mountain rain, a persistent, soaking downpour, rattling the roof tiles, gurgling from the down-spouts and thrumming on the marble paving of the piazza. The weather has cast a feeling of gloom over all the New Year's Eve festivities.

Pia gives Matteo a shake. 'Time to wake up, *caro*.' He grunts and turns over. He's very fond of sleep. Pia thinks it's because he can escape all his problems when he's unconscious; his father Enzo, the situation in the bar, and

– of course – herself.

On New Year's Eve the bar is open all night, so it's important to get some rest before the celebrations begin at ten thirty. In the early evening Italian families eat together before coming out to celebrate the 'Fine d'Anno'. She and Matteo had had a quick pizza together at six o'clock. There was no way that Matteo could be persuaded to eat at the house of his father and his stepmother, and Pia – as a mere employee – would never be invited, so they'd eaten one of Franco's 'specials' together in the empty bar, like two companions in exile, before going to bed.

As Pia towels herself dry after the shower, she looks out of the window onto the wet piazza. It's almost empty and the rain dazzles on the marble tiles as the puddles reflect the Christmas lights. Below the window, heavy pockets of water have formed in the canvas awning over the entrance to the bar. Further away, beyond the Duomo steps, the floodlights illuminate the Michelangelo tower where two men are placing cables in the doorway.

Things are just beginning to happen. The sound guys are working on the covered stage where the band will be performing later. Every now and then there's a booming 'Uno, due, tre' and the electric whine of feedback.

Taj, the Tibetan busker, has already taken up his position in the doorway of the Bank of Rapallo with his rabbit in its cage beside him, protected by a plastic bag, and the scruffy Alsatian dog stretched out at his feet.

Pia can see Babacar, the Senegalese street trader, already standing outside Franco's pizzeria. He's erected a big beach umbrella to protect himself and his wares from the rain. He's hung about with beads and belts and fake designer handbags, with a pyramid of hats on his head, like a walking market stall. Tonight one arm is also hooked with umbrella handles. Babacar's dark skin blends so perfectly with the darkness that all she can see clearly is the glitter of belt buckles and the light reflecting from the wheel of cigarette lighters that he carries slung across his chest like a warrior's shield.

Then, round the corner of the piazza, comes the old midwife, the woman everyone calls Nonna, because she does seem to be everyone's grandmother, if not in fact, by right of having been there at the birth. Nonna's face is very white under the lights and from up here Pia can look down on her head, which is almost bald, except for a long, thin, coil of reddish hair wound round her pink scalp. She's carrying a bowl of something and, as Pia watches, she goes over to the Bank of Rapallo and puts it down in front of the Tibetan's dog.

Pia turns away from the window. 'Matteo! It's nearly half past.'

He groans, but rolls over and throws himself out of bed where he stands naked, stretching and yawning for a moment before going into the bathroom.

Pia switches on the hair dryer and ruffles her short curls with one hand to speed up the drying process. She has indigestion. Perhaps from eating the pizza too quickly. Or perhaps from something else. Just considering that possibility makes Pia feel nauseous. If she really *is*, what's going to happen to her? Matteo, who is now singing lustily under the shower head, is not to be relied on, and their relationship so new and fragile it could break under the pressure.

Downstairs Eva is coating tiny pieces of bread with paté and spearing them with a slice of gherkin. 'You're late!' she says, slamming the knife down on the marble work surface.

21

Eva is taller than Pia and ten years older, with coarse hair streaked blonde and worn pinned up on top of her head. She has well-formed breasts that Pia envies. Eva is *'una donna forte'*.

'What can I do?' Pia has already put on her black apron with the Bar di Pietro logo across it. The bar is actually owned by Enzo, Matteo's father. No one seems to know who Pietro was, or if he has ever existed.

Eva gestures to the trays of bar snacks. 'You can put them on the counter and then we need some fruit sliced up for the drinks – there'll be no time to do that later. *Porca misere*! Why does it have to rain for New Year. Everyone will be trying to come inside – it will be *un casino*!' She throws up her hands to show what she thinks of chaos.

The door clicks open. 'We're closed until ten thirty,' Eva calls out. But it's only the Milanese woman, Anastasia, with her crazy dog Fidel.

'I came to say *Auguri*,' she says. 'Is Matteo here?'

'He's upstairs getting dressed. Would you like a drink?' Pia asks. 'We can make an exception for you!'

'No, thank you.' Rain is dripping off the hem of Anastasia's coat and from Fidel's long ears, which he shakes energetically, sending arcs of raindrops across the bar. 'I've just brought him out for a quick trot before it gets busy and now I'm taking him home so we can have a night cap together and watch TV.'

'Aren't you going to come out and celebrate?'

Anastasia shakes her head. 'I can't leave him – he gets so distressed, even with a sedative.'

She looks unhappy. Pia wonders whether she has enough money for a drink. Lately she's been ordering *spuma bionda* – the cheapest thing they have.

'You shouldn't have offered her anything,' Eva

22

says, after Anastasia has disappeared back into the rain. 'We're too busy.'

Pia can do nothing right here. She knows that Eva doesn't like her. Eva is Italian; Pia is only a Greek immigrant – an economic migrant – without proper papers. And Eva knows that Enzo doesn't approve of his son sharing the room above the bar with Pia. Sleeping with the boss's son should count for something, Pia thinks, but Eva's influence counts for much, much more. Pia knows the reason why she has to work all the shitty shifts. Matteo is supposed to be the manager of the bar, but everyone knows the situation. He's only in charge until Enzo appears bellowing 'Matteo!' ready to list some crime his son has committed, or something essential he's overlooked.

Pia is sure Eva is having an affair with Enzo – she purrs like a cat when he's around, and is bad-tempered when he's not. Pia doesn't envy her. Enzo's second wife, Hilaria, has him constantly under surveillance.

There's a smug, self-satisfied expression on Eva's face tonight and Pia notices that she's wearing the Louboutin shoes. They had appeared on Christmas Eve – the bag dropped casually on the bar like a boast, just begging everyone to ask for a glimpse of the dark blue leather with red lacquered insteps, glittering crystal ankle straps and more crystals embedded on the tapering heels. When Eva had tried them on, tottering across the uneven surface of the bar in exquisite agony, they had brought squeals of delight and envy from the beautiful girls who paraded their elegant bodies around the piazza during the *passeggiata*. At least four hundred euros, Pia calculates, possibly more, so how could a mere *barista* afford those shoes unless they were a gift from someone?

Matteo is running down the stairs. His damp hair

is slicked up in peaks on the top of his head and he looks unbelievably cute. Pia's stomach turns over with love for him and he smiles at her – a very private smile that seems to say everything he can't put into words. He flicks on the stereo and spins the dial on the iPod. It's Fabrizio de Andre, sentimental, slightly melancholy, and it suits Pia's mood perfectly.

'I'll start making the punch,' Matteo says to Eva and he picks up a bottle of Aperol, reaches down a bottle of orange syrup and another of grappa from the shelf and slips through the bamboo curtain into the tiny kitchen at the back.

Eva gives Pia a *Look*.

I'm an economic migrant, Pia reminds herself. I don't have the proper papers, my boss does not approve of my relationship with his son, and I must be very careful because I need this job.

Her parents live in Piraeus and since the crisis they have had no work. Her father had been a fisherman until the accident that had broken his leg; her mother has a heart condition and can no longer clean in the local hotel. The money Pia sends them every month is supposed to put bread and fish on the table, though Pia is afraid some of it's wasted on her father's taste for *raki*.

The door bangs open. It's Enzo, cursing and shaking his umbrella. He's a big, muscular man carrying a little too much weight for his height. His hair is improbably blonde and fluffed around his face by a clever hairdresser to hide the burgeoning bald spot on the crown of his head. He ignores Pia, pats Eva on the shoulder and yells 'Matteo!'

'He's making the punch,' Eva says.

On New Year's Eve it's apparently the tradition to serve a cauldron of hot punch outside in plastic cups in order to cope with the crowds of people that gather in the piazza for the festivities. This is Pia's first New Year's Eve here and she doesn't quite know what to expect.

'Switch off that wailing,' Enzo says, pointing to Pia. 'Put something cheerful on – it's the end of the year, not the end of the world.' He laughs at his own joke.

Pia spins the dial. There's a play list called 'celebration'. She presses Select and the electric beat of American rock begins to pulsate across the room.

Twenty five past ten. The door opens and it's the English sculptor they call Martin – Pia doesn't know his surname, there are only first names in the bar. Pia has been told he's quite famous, but she's never heard of him. Tonight Martin has the slightly smudged look of someone who has already had a great deal to drink and he wades across the bar as if swimming through air.

'*Auguri tutti!*' he calls. At least a cheerful drunk.

'*Auguri*, Martin.' Pia finds a smile. 'What would you like?'

'Campari bitter, but no ice. You don't need ice on a night like this.'

Pia swings the Campari bottle over the sliced lemon and then holds the glass briefly under the syphon before putting it down on the bar in front of him. 'Three fifty please.'

He looks surprised.

'There's no time to run a tab tonight – everyone has to pay when they order. Sorry.'

Martin wriggles his fingers deep into his pockets but only finds a handful of change which he spills on the counter. Mainly small coins and Pia has to count out the correct amount for him. She tries hard to be patient.

25

Behind Martin a crowd of people, boisterous and laughing, undaunted by the rain, wrestle themselves in through the narrow door, bringing eddies of cold air with their damp clothes. Matteo has put a plastic bin beside the door and it's already full of umbrellas. There's no stopping now. 'Three red wines and a gin and tonic – four Campari spritz – two Margaritas – a Russian cocktail – one Fernot Branca – a Negroni – three proseccos – two Aperol spritz' – the lists sing in Pia's head and she performs to them as if it's a dance. Reach up for the glass, then turn for the bottle, drink on the bar, money in the till. Eva and Matteo stretch and bend on either side of her, avoiding each other with practised choreography.

After the first rush is over, Enzo and Matteo take the cauldron of punch out to the piazza and put it on the burner next to the wooden table they've erected. The awning over them drips and gushes unexpectedly as the rain keeps falling. Babacar is still standing under his umbrella at the corner, waving at everyone who comes past him. 'You need umbrella? I give you nice price.' Most people have already got one but he's undeterred. 'That is not very nice umbrella – I give you better one. Nice price.'

Matteo puts his hand on Pia's arm. 'Can you take him a glass of tea and a plate of snacks? He likes a lot of sugar in his tea.'

She nods.

'And don't let Papa see you. He'd kill us!'

Pia slips out of the back door with the glass and a plastic plate with some *focaccia* and a selection of *crostini* on it.

'For you, Babacar – from Matteo.'

'Thank you. Thank you.' Babacar leans his umbrellas against the wall before he takes the plate and the glass from her. 'That is very nice. *Auguri!*' His whole face beams at her. 'I wish you very good things for this year – you and Matteo!'

Pia tries to smile, but she feels like crying. 'Thank you Babacar. We hope so too. *Auguri. Buon anno!*'

She turns to go back into the bar. The band are just tuning up on stage. It's all just about to begin, but Pia doesn't even dare to think of the coming year.

On the other corner, Stefania is standing at the pizza stall – the pizzeria is selling them only by the slice tonight – and as Pia passes, Franco is just staggering out with another laden tray.

'For God's sake,' Pia hears Stefania say, 'These are burnt at the edges! You want me to sell these?'

'The oven is too hot – I left them in one moment too long.' Franco shrugs and wipes his hands on his overall.

'You have too much grappa in you!' Pia hears her say in a bitter *sotto voce*.

'It is *Capo d'Anno*! What do you expect?'

Stefania turns her back and begins cutting up the pizzas.

There's a screech of electronic noise. The PA system has been switched on and Pia turns for a moment to look at the man in a grey suit, standing in the centre of the stage holding a microphone. 'Hello everyone! Hello!' He waits for people to stop talking and then begins again. 'Welcome. Thank you for coming to help us celebrate the birth of a new year. In a moment we have music from' – he consults a piece of paper – 'No Panic,' he pronounces the words carefully waving an arm towards the musicians behind him. 'I'm sure you are all waiting to hear this amazing new band from Bologna,' he pauses for a spatter of applause and some impatient whistles from the crowd. 'But first we have a few words from our *Sindaco*!'

A short, bald-headed man wearing the green, red and white mayoral sash of office steps up to the microphone. He clears his throat. The sound echoes around the piazza. Pia can hear Enzo snort behind her – 'Self-important little bastard.'

Matteo has told her that his father intends to run for *Sindaco* next year when the current mayor's term is over. You need money to get elected, money and connections. The current incumbent has a construction business – 'Dug his way in with a pick and shovel,' Enzo says, whenever anyone mentions his name in the bar.

Pia is surprised to find Italy at least as corrupt as Greece. Everything here is done 'on the black' – even her wages are cash-in-hand out of the till and not in Enzo's books. This means that technically she has no job and can never get a work permit or certificate of residence. Officially she doesn't exist, like Babacar, or the Albanian boys who live in the parking lot.

Matteo has tried to talk to Enzo about it, but he won't listen. There are a hundred young girls like herself out there looking for any kind of work. And she's lucky. Almost half of Italy's young people would kill for a job that isn't seasonal. The opportunity mustn't be thrown away. It's the same circumstance that keeps Matteo as his father's slave, though they are barely on speaking terms. Matteo has told her that their hostility goes back a long way, from the time when Enzo had left his mother. He hadn't treated her well. Matteo is very fond of his mother, though she no longer lives here. His differences with Enzo are both personal and political.

'You know he has Mussolini's cap hanging on the

wall of his study at home?' Matteo had said once.

'He's a fascist?'

Matteo nodded. 'Still goes boar hunting with the same group whose fathers used to hunt partisans at the end of the war. Here you're either a fascist or a communist. Centre right or centre left.'

'And you?'

'I'm nothing. Religion and politics – I don't want to have anything to do with either.' There's something a little too diplomatic about Matteo – a little too compliant. Lately he's taken up meditation in order to maintain a peaceful spirit. It isn't natural, Pia thinks, for anyone to be so calm. Be angry! She wants to say to him. Fight for what you want!

Eleven thirty. The music has begun. It's impossible to hear anyone order drinks over the booming thump thump of the rock beat, but mercifully there's a lull as everyone pushes outside to watch. Pia goes to the door for a breath of air. They're playing some Rolling Stones numbers now and suddenly there's a disturbance on the stage. Franco has climbed up. He's wearing a blond wig and miming Mick Jagger to the bemusement of the band who don't know that this is Franco's Saturday night party-piece in the pizzeria. They are from Bologna and don't know that the restaurant is decorated with photographs, posters, record sleeves and every kind of Stones' memorabilia. Franco grabs a microphone from one of the stands. There are a few cat-calls and some booing. 'Perleese,' Franco yells into the mike. 'You are brrreaking my balls!' There are shouts of laughter across the piazza as he continues to gyrate. Pia can see two security men moving in his direction.

'He's pissed again,' Eva says. 'Stefania will be

furious.'

'She already is. He burned the pizzas.'

Eva laughs. She seems in a better humour now. 'Then he's a marked man. This is not going to be his year. There are rumours.'

Eva and Matteo are handing out cups of punch at the front of the bar, two euros a shot, and the pile of coins in the plastic box is growing steadily. The bar is quieter and Pia takes the opportunity to clear the glasses and load the dishwasher. As she bends down to insert the tray into the machine, Enzo comes up behind her and runs his hand casually over her buttocks, pressing a finger, expertly, between them as he does so. It only takes a few seconds, but she feels outraged. He often does things like this. Pia hasn't said anything to Matteo, but she's afraid to be alone with Enzo, because she fears that he would do more if there was no-one there to restrain him.

The rain stops in time for the fireworks at twelve. Enzo locks the door and they all stand outside looking up at the colourful bursts of electric stars shooting miraculously from the top of the Michelangelo tower to illuminate the grey cloud ceiling still hanging ominously over them. The banging and cracking of the fireworks, the music from the stage and the joyful pealing of bells in the campanile drown out the calls of *'Auguri! Buon anno!'* around the piazza. It's already January. A new year. Through the crowds Pia glimpses Franco slumped on one of the pizzeria tables, his blond wig pushed to the side.

Matteo is standing behind her. He puts his arms around her and murmurs against her ear that everything will be okay. He kisses the back of her neck. *'Amore,'* he says. Everyone is jumping up and down, hugging and kissing each other in an orgy of gladness and optimism. But Pia doesn't feel happy. There is such fear in her throat she thinks she might choke on it.

2

The Midwife's Story

They're always nervous when they come for the first time. Clara observes how the girl sits, upright on the wooden chair, her hands doing some work of their own on her lap, her gaze darting here and there around the room. Her face is familiar, but she's not one of the flock of beautiful, fashionable girls who gather in the piazza during the *passeggiata*. Not beautiful, or fashionable, but nevertheless, this girl has something about her; the cropped dark hair, high cheekbones, and skin the colour of cream. Clara knows why she's come; these girls always have a look – something in the eyes, a little more fullness around the jawbone perhaps – but so far this girl has said nothing apart from conversational pleasantries. Her Italian is good, although she has a strong accent that Clara can't place.

'You're not from here?' Clara says. She has plenty of time. She can wait.

The girl hesitates and then says, 'From Greece. There was no work there.' She shrugs her shoulders in a 'what could I do?' gesture. 'My parents are old – they need me to send money.'

'I think I've seen you working in the bar downstairs.'

The girl nods. 'Sometimes. And sometimes at the

beach. Enzo owns another bar in Forte dei Marmi and I worked there all the time when I was first here. I came with a friend, but then she met a boy and went to America.'

'You also have a boyfriend?'

The girl blushes and lowers her head.

Clara waits for a moment and then says, as gently as she can, 'Do you think now, you could tell me why you've come?'

The girl looks up, her eyes are glossy with tears. 'I am afraid . . . I might be pregnant.'

Clara smiles at her. 'Is that so terrible?'

'If you are not married, and the man you love only does what his father tells him . . .'

'Matteo?'

She nods again.

'He's a good boy, you know. It's only that he's afraid of his father – many people in this town are. Everyone knows that in Enzo's house, in his private office, he has a signed photograph of *Il Duce* that was given to his own father. It's a shrine to Mussolini. Why do you think Enzo's dog is called Beni?'

'Oh! I thought it was Benny – like the American cartoon.' The girl is looking more relaxed now.

Clara smiles. 'Matteo's grandfather was a big fascist during the war – that's how the family got so much property and land. But Matteo takes after his mother – she was a very gentle girl, educated by the nuns, one of the old kind.'

'You knew her?'

'I delivered all her children, even Matteo.'

The girl's expression changes. 'People say that you still practise. Can you help me?'

It's a question Clara has heard often from girls

who are desperate, but she has, almost always, said no. There are other ways; she has always tried to keep them out of the convent, out of the clutches of the nuns, if she can. Clara has never known why it should be a crime to bring a baby into the world without a husband. Hadn't the Blessed Virgin herself conceived a child outside wedlock – and not with her *fidanzato*? Better to stay away from the nuns. There are families desperate for a child who would gladly offer a refuge for a girl in trouble in return for the gift of a baby. Sometimes there's a distant relative who can take the girl in, and then there's a sympathetic priest in Genoa who runs a refuge for victims of incest.

Clara knows all about incest. In those high villages up on the shoulders of the marble mountains, where life went on as it had for a thousand years, families in crowded houses, sharing beds. Grandmothers had their young grandsons in their beds with them, young girls shared rooms with their grandfathers, separated by only a thin cotton curtain. Fathers and daughters, brothers and sisters. Nothing could ever surprise or shock her now, and no-one would ever get her to reveal the strange webs of relationship, tacitly understood but never talked about, in those mountainous hamlets.

Clara levers herself upright on the edge of the table. 'First we must find out if you are right. Come and lie down here.' Clara indicates the wooden day bed near the stove, the bed that had been her mother's. 'When did you last see your monthly friend?'

The girl screws up her eyes as if to calculate. 'It was due just before Christmas, but it didn't come – and then last month, January, it didn't come again. I should have used one of those kits from the *Farmacia*, but I was afraid someone would see me buying one, or maybe Matteo would find it in the bathroom.'

Clara waits until the girl stretches herself out on the quilt and lifts her T-shirt. The zip of her jeans is already undone, held together with a length of ribbon. Clara probes softly just above the pubic bone, seeking out the first swelling of the womb under her fingers. Then she straightens up. 'Nearly three months, I think. So yes, you are going to have a child.'

The girl shields her eyes with her arm and begins to sob. Clara puts a hand on her shoulder and grips it for a moment, before moving to the stove to light the gas under the kettle. 'A *tisane*? You should not drink coffee now, it's bad for the *bambino*.'

The girl is wiping her face with some tissues from her bag. 'Will you help me?' she asks again. Her face is full of grief.

'I will help you to have the baby, but I'll have no part in killing it – for that you will need to go to the doctor at the hospital and make an appointment. But you must think very carefully before you do that. This is Matteo's baby too. A little life he is also responsible for.' She pours the boiling water into the pot with the tea bags. 'Who knows, perhaps this is what he needs to become a man and stand up to his father?'

'He'll never do that. I've watched him.' The girl takes the cup that Clara is holding out. 'I'm so afraid.' She puts her hand over her mouth and a drop of tea spills onto the table top.

Clara reaches across the table to touch the girl's arm. 'There's no need. It's the most natural thing in the world. This is what we are here for – to make babies. It's beautiful.'

The girl tries to smile. 'It doesn't feel like that

now.'

'But when you have your baby in your arms and it opens its eyes and you see yourself reflected in them – then you will understand.'

Clara has watched that epiphany many times – seen the revelation light up their faces, and felt a gladness wash over herself, a glow of love and wonder, that was like nothing else she had ever experienced.

There's a sudden clatter from behind the loggia door, a thrumming and beating sound. Then silence.

'What's that?' The girl looks alarmed. 'Is there someone else here?'

'It's only the pigeons. They are my companions. My son left, you know, and after he went away I began to look after them, feed them, give them medicine when they are sick. They roost on my balcony and they know that it's safe to lay their eggs there. Come and see.' She opens the door onto the loggia. In the dim light, rows and rows of eyes glint red from the birds perching in lines along the stone rail and the ledges of the wall.

The girl has pinched her nostrils together with her fingers. 'How can you stand the smell?' she asks. 'Why do you do it?'

'People are so unkind. They treat them badly and sometimes they put poison in their food. No-one takes the time to see how beautiful they are.' Clara thinks they are among the most beautiful of birds, with all the subtle greys of their feathers and the shawl of peacock colours round their necks. She holds out her hand and one of them flies across the loggia and settles on her wrist. Clara strokes its head with a finger. She offers it to the girl.

'Here, touch, feel its heart beating.'

But the girl recoils.

'They are very intelligent you know. The Holy Spirit came to earth as a pigeon, and it was a pigeon that found the first land after the Great Flood. They are very clever birds.'

The girl seems unconvinced. Back in the kitchen she stops in front of a photograph on the dresser. 'This is your husband?'

'Yes, that was my Tommaso. He had a hard life, working in the quarry. Have you never wondered why we are all widows in this town?' Clara picks up the photograph and touches his face gently. 'It's because the men are killed by work – the quarries are very dangerous – cutting the big marble blocks, swinging them on the cranes, driving them down the mountain on those perilous roads. If they don't get killed by accident, they burst their hearts heaving the marble out. In those days they used to blow a steam whistle when there was an accident. We would hear the whistle and wonder who was being brought down. That was a terrible moment.'

'Is that what happened to your husband?'

Clara shakes her head. 'Tommaso became a cutter, sawing up the blocks of marble. He breathed the dust every day of his working life and in the end it filled his lungs and he died.'

'I'm sorry.'

'*Sai com'è.* It's how life is.' Clara puts the photograph back on the dresser. 'But I grieve for my son.' She takes another image down from the shelf. A boy with dark, curly hair and dark, almost gypsy skin, swarthy like his father. A serious expression.

'What happened?' the girl asks.

'Perhaps you have noticed that tall, blonde girl who comes here sometimes? The Danish sculptress? He was

mad for her, so when she went back to her own country he
followed her there and I have never heard from him since.
I see her sometimes in the piazza when she's here, but she
says she doesn't know where he is. I am sure she's lying.
Why would he not want to talk to his mother? It makes
me very sad.'

Clara wakes suddenly in the chair by the stove and can
hear steps echoing on the stairs. It can't be the girl because
Clara can remember her leaving. There's a banging on her
door. and then it opens and Nico is standing there with his
arms full of logs. Two of the other Albanian boys are on
the landing behind him, sweating under the weight of the
wood.

'You want it all inside, Nonna?' Nico says. 'Or we
leave it here?'

'Some of it here and some of it there,' Clara
says, gesticulating. One must speak very simply with the
Albanian boys.

While they stack the wood, Clara puts the coffee
pot on the stove and takes down a new *panettone* from the
shelf. Not the one flavoured with grappa – they are all
Muslims. Four coffee cups and three plates.

'*Come state?*' she asks when they are all seated round the
table. 'How does it go?'

'Good, good.' It's always Nico who answers.
The two younger ones don't speak much Italian. Despite
working most of the time outdoors they have pale, clean
skin that contrasts with their glossy black hair and jet black
eyes. Nico has always been different, since he came when
he was sixteen – the leader of the group, the spokesperson.
Clara had been there when someone got drunk in the bar

and began to call them names, abusing their religion, and she had seen him stop one of the younger ones getting out of his seat to attack the man. Nico had grabbed him by the collar and pushed him down again, shouting at him in their own language. And then he had made them all leave. They had no money in those days and slept in the courtyard of the Misericordia.

'How are the caravans?' Clara asks.

The boys smile.

'They are good, good,' Nico says. 'Father Hermes comes every week to see. He is very nice, for an *arabo*.'

Clara thinks it's odd for an Albanian to discriminate against an Arab, but then, Father Hermes is a Christian. There is prejudice everywhere, even among refugees.

'And you get plenty of work?'

'Yes, yes. Last month it was hard, but now there is a little. This week we clear an old house for the owner to make tourist place. Next week we paint.'

They have the reputation of being hard workers. They strim the grass in the olive groves in forty degrees of summer heat; they repair the paths on the mountain when temperatures are below zero and no self-respecting Italian will venture up there; they prune olive trees and put the tiles back on people's roofs. Any job that does not require official papers. And they can get you anything, on the black, if you ask. Only God and the Albanian boys know where her wood has come from, but it keeps her fire stoked all winter.

'I get some work at the gym now,' Nico says. 'I help people make muscle like mine.' He flashes a white grin and flexes his biceps to show her. He has broad muscular shoulders and long arms.

Clara doesn't ask them personal questions any

more. When they had first arrived, thin and hungry, and she had invited them into her kitchen and given them bowls of bean soup, she had asked them about their families and they had all fallen silent. The youngest one had cried. So now she doesn't ask.

In the evening Clara likes to sit in the piazza and watch the *passeggiata*. It's cool in February, but Franco and Matteo have those gas heaters like metal flowers, radiating heat between the tables. She doesn't have any particular preference for one bar or the other, but at the moment Clara is sitting in the Bar di Pietro. Matteo has some of last season's good red wine from the *cantina*, which is mellowing gently – you can still taste the grapes and something of the summer sun in the full red liquid.

She always sits in the back corner near the door. The families are all making their promenade. There are no tourists in February and Clara knows almost everyone. The Milanese woman, Anastasia, is there with her dog. The Baldacchinis stroll past in their finery, towards the Enoteca. The *Avvocato* buys his clothes in Florence; his wife buys hers in Rome. She is too thin for her age, which makes her face harsh. Her lips pout – Clara thinks that she goes to the beauty clinic to be injected. And the woman is tottering on designer shoes, the heels too high for her – all this torture just to keep that expensive bag of wind walking beside her. But they are still together after more than thirty years, so that is perhaps something.

Clara has been sitting here, first with her mother and then with her husband, since she was a young girl – nearly seventy years. But there is a certain sadness now about the view. Once the piazza had been full of the kind of shops ordinary people like herself would use. On the corner, where the *gelateria* is now, there was a lace shop owned by a French-Italian woman who was *molto simpatica*. She used to sit every day on a chair outside with her lace pillow and chat to everyone while she twirled the little silver bobbins on the white linen. Next to the *gelateria*, there's a designer clothes boutique that was once a vegetable shop run by a brother and a sister – though Maria was the boss with the money and the sales – Hugo just carried the boxes and dug the vegetables out of the ground. And there had been a book shop, a bakery and a tool shop. Now they have all become exclusive boutiques and restaurants and art galleries. There is nowhere for people to buy their bread or their groceries. There are glossy supermarkets on the outskirts of town, but it isn't possible for Clara to carry the shopping home across such a distance. If it wasn't for the weekly market in the piazza, life would be very difficult.

A little boy of five or six pedals up to Clara on his bicycle. He has long curly hair almost down to his shoulders, like a girl. He smiles up at her without saying anything.

'Paolo! How you've grown! Where is Mama?'

Paolo points across at Franco's – Simona is sitting with a group of young people; some of the beautiful girls and the Albanian boys. She's smoking and has her back to the piazza. Clara feels annoyed – someone should be looking out for the child.

'How is your school?'

The boy makes a face.

'Would you like an ice cream? An *aranciata*?'

He smiles broadly.

'*Va bene*! But first you must tell your mother where you are, and then you must put your bicycle against the wall.'

As she orders the *gelato* and the fizzy drink, Clara tries not to think of the fate that had given her only one child and yet gave children freely to girls who did not want them and could not care for them. But she has long since stopped trying to understand the Mysteries. God, no doubt, has some plan, hidden from the eyes of ordinary mortals.

The Tibetan man is there, playing his long Alpenhorn, making a mournful, wailing sound that echoes around the piazza. He has his belongings on a wheeled luggage trolley beside him, with his rabbit in a cage and the dog stretched out on the marble tiles at his feet.

After Paolo has eaten his ice cream and gone back to pedalling his aimless circles around the piazza, Clara walks across to where the Tibetan is still honking into his instrument. When you go near him, there's a strong smell of incense and marijuana. Clara knows that smell – her son had had a plastic bag of it at the back of the wardrobe, which she had found after he had gone, and she had recognised the strange smell that was sometimes on his clothes.

She bends to pat the big Alsatian, saying 'Good evening, Louis' in a soothing voice. The dog feels thin under her fingers. She drops a euro into the tin in front of him.

The Tibetan puts down the wooden tube and gets out his pipe. 'You know they have a petition to take him away from me and put him in the *Canile?*'

Clara says nothing, since she is the one who has made the *denuncia.*

Taj is lighting his pipe. 'They say I don't look after him. My only companion. My friend. I care for him as I would my mother or my father.'

'You don't feed him enough, Taj.'

He shrugs. 'I share my food with him. Is it my fault there's so little? What will I do without him? He keeps me warm at night and he stops those idiot boys from pestering me.'

'Where are you sleeping now? It's too cold to sleep in the street.'

'At the back of the church. Father Hermes allows me, but the other priests don't like it – bugger them! *Vaffanculo*! They say I am not Catholic, I am Buddhist, so I have no place there and especially not the dog. But Hermes says that Saint Francis allowed animals into church, so when he is there it's okay.'

'Can he not get you one of the caravans?'

Taj gave a grunt of distaste. 'I can't live in a tin box. I need air! I like to have space around me, to see the mountains and the stars. I told him no.'

'Well, I will do what I can, Taj. But I am eighty two, you know. I am not what I was.'

Before she goes to bed, Clara always goes to the Baptistry. She feels more at home there than in the Duomo. Clara has always loved the big, octagonal marble font, the painted, domed ceiling overhead, the Madonna in her blue robes with her baby cradled in her arms and her calm, sad smile.

Clara dips her fingers in the holy water and makes the sign of the cross. Once, when she came in, there had been a young girl, sitting out of sight in a dark corner, and she had been singing in the language of the mass – Clara doesn't know about music, but it had seemed to come from a long time ago. There was an unearthly beauty in the shape of the strange harmonies that echoed round the

44

marble walls, so that it sounded like a whole choir, chords and single notes that had thrilled her in some primitive way. The sensation was so strong it had shocked her.

And she had remembered the day she had first seen the man she would marry. It had been her father's funeral, after he'd been killed in the quarry and Tommaso had come because they'd worked together in the same team, winding and levering the heavy blocks up on wooden rollers to get them down the slope to the trucks. Clara remembered looking through her tears and seeing a tall boy with dark curly hair that needed cutting. A serious boy with a delicate face. He had looked at her and taken her hand and said, 'I'm sorry. He was a good man.' And something had entered her and stuck in her heart and she had trembled all over. Later she'd told the secret to her sister, because Maria couldn't tell or remember anything – 'That is the man I am going to marry.'

After her father's death the *comune* had given Clara's mother the apartment in the piazza; a widow with five children and one of them an idiot, damaged at birth because the midwife hadn't known what to do. It was Maria who had given Clara her purpose. When their father died, Clara had been the eldest and it was her duty to earn money to keep the family until her brothers were old enough to work, and somehow she had known that she must train as a midwife, with as much medical knowledge as she could get, to save women from the kind of ignorance that had produced Maria. Tommaso had had to wait for her, and then he had had to carry on living with her mother and her sister after her brothers left home. Now, out of them all, only one of them is still alive apart from herself.

Georgio had gone to America and sends postcards of children and grandchildren Clara doesn't recognise.

45

She thinks sometimes of the siblings she has lost; little Francesco killed on his bicycle outside the school when he was nine; Fabrizio felled by a stroke in the car factory in Milan at forty-two. Maria had not lived beyond twenty-five – a blessing, Clara supposes, but it had left a gap. Her mother had missed that child more than any of the others. There was a saying she had – 'A son's a son till he finds a wife; a daughter's a daughter for life'. Clara had always tried to be a good daughter as well as a good wife and mother. But Tommaso had died, from the pneumonia, so suddenly, so unexpectedly, and – after their son Marco had left – there had been only her mother, lying on the cot beside the stove, with no more sensibility than a six month old child. And now Clara is alone.

When Clara opens the door the apartment seems very empty. The stove is ticking in the corner. She opens it and puts in another log. The green wood hisses and spits.

And then the rain begins – a sound like breathing outside the window, then pattering like birds' feet on the roof. Clara pulls back the glass and opens the shutters to gaze down on the brightly lit piazza. The marble paving has a glossy sheen where the light falls. People are moving to and fro as if engaged in a complicated dance with each other, on their way home from the restaurants. There's a sudden flowering of colour as they unfurl their umbrellas. She can see Babacar, the Senegalese street trader, materialising from a side street like a magician wheeling a suitcase sprouting handles, brandishing one of his cheap Chinese umbrellas towards anyone who doesn't have one.

There's the glow of a cigarette from the dark shadow outside the kitchen door of Franco's Pizzeria. 'There's a man with trouble in his heart,' Clara thinks.

She's been watching Stefania. A man wants a wife, but then a wife wants a child. That is the way of things. *Dio abbia pietà di noi.* May God have mercy.

3

Babacar

Babacar is walking along a dirt road. The red dust irritates his feet, so he has taken off his sandals and strung them round his neck. There are thorn trees on either side of the track and a cow with protruding hip bones is carefully pulling off any leaves it can reach with its tongue.

In the distance Babacar can see the rusting corrugated tin roofs of his village. He feels as though he's been walking for a long time, but the houses never get any closer. The sun is like a heavy weight on his back and the top of his head. He seems to be carrying luggage.

A small boy, dressed in a cotton shift, is herding two or three goats with a stick. He could be Babacar's son. How old is he – about eight? How is it possible not to recognise your own child? He calls 'Omar!' But the boy turns and looks at him and then runs away.

The village has gone – there's only a heat haze dissolving the road into mirage, or perhaps it's the beginning of a *shamaal* – already little swirls of dust are leaping into the air, dancing among the thorn trees like dervishes.

'Omar!' Babacar shouts. 'Omar! It's your father. Don't run!'

He wakes with a jerk. A drop of condensation has fallen from the ceiling onto his face. He wipes it off with a corner of the blanket. The darkness is thick with human sweat, farts and the musty odour of the black mould that has crept over the walls and ceiling during the winter. All around him men are grunting and snoring in their sleep, curled on either side of him on their bedrolls – nine of them in this one room. But at least they keep each other warm.

No-one, when they talked about how wonderful it was in Europe, had told him about the winter cold. The summer heat he can cope with – the *Gran Caldo* – but the freezing temperatures are something else. And the damp. It gets into the joints and makes the blood congeal in your arteries.

Selim, the gangmaster, arrives at six. Even in winter the markets begin early. He bangs on all the doors, shouting '*Yallah! Yallah!*' Selim has brought the two women with him and they make breakfast in the tiny kitchen illuminated by a single, dim bulb and the grey, slushy light filtering through the shutters. Corn porridge, though they call it *polenta* here, and it's not bad with a little of the juice of last night's chicken on it. Babacar misses the food from home – there is fish and rice here, but it's not *Tiboudienne*. You can't get the spices, or the right kind of rice.

Selim is handing out the orders for today. 'Jawa - you take the flowers down to the station. Abdou and Farid, I want you outside the Conad.'

There's a murmur from the back of the room. The supermarket car park isn't a favourite pitch because of the competition from the Roma, who return shoppers' trolleys and harass them for coins. Because of that, many people make a blind run between their cars and the door. It's difficult to sell anything there.

Babacar is to go to the little market in the piazza, as

he usually does. Some of the others are going to the more expensive designer market at Forte dei Marmi. Mostly the *Marocchini*, Babacar observes. Selim is a *Marocchino* – tall and thin in his *djellaba*, with one gold tooth and an embroidered cap on his shaven head. There's friction among the men because they think he gives better pitches to his own countrymen than he does to the Senegalese.

As he rides in the back of the van to town, Babacar's thoughts are on how to gain his independence. It's eighteen months now since Selim had found him sitting on the steps of the railway station wondering where to go and what to do. Since then things haven't changed at all. Babacar sells well, better than the others – people seem to like him – but Selim takes the money and in return gives Babacar his bed and board in the overcrowded house. Like the others, Babacar keeps back a percentage of what he makes for pocket money and, so long as his take from the goods is reasonable, Selim asks no questions. But a few euros here and there aren't enough to pay for a passage back to Senegal, or buy a ticket for his wife and children. Selim, on the other hand, has a Mercedes parked at the back of his villa, two wives, four or five servants and a flock of children. But then, he's a *Marocchino*, not a *Wolof*.

Selim drops him at the entrance to the piazza. Babacar hasn't said anything about the bicycle. One of the American sculptors from the studio had given it to Babacar when he left, the last time. 'Keep it for me,' he'd said. 'If I ever come back you can return it.' Babacar keeps the bike chained in the rack at the station. It means he doesn't always have to ride in the van with the others; he can go to the markets in some of the little villages to make extra money. And sometimes he leaves his pack in the Misericordia and cycles down to the sea just to stand there and look at it.

The Mediterranean is quieter and better behaved than the ocean in Senegal where the waves roll in with the whole weight of the Atlantic crashing behind them. Somewhere over there, across the glittering blue water, are his wife N'gof and his children, Omar, Fatou and Baby Mirabelle. It's a pain under Babacar's heart to think that he may never see them again. He doesn't go down to the sea very often because of the memories it brings of his arrival in Italy, after the long journey across the desert. He had been promised papers, a job – he'd saved for more than a year to get the money to come here, to make a better life for his family.

He still has nightmares about the overloaded boat – the sea that glittered until his head swam with bits of light like broken glass, the thirst that swelled his tongue until it split open his mouth. Then the launches, skittering over the sea towards them, drenching the occupants with warm spray. The hands reaching down to take him – rubber gloves on their hands. They wore blue suits and masks as if they would be contaminated by contact with such vermin.

The detention centre was a concrete bunker surrounded by wire, but it was full so they were taken to a derelict school building. Babacar was amazed to find that he was only one among hundreds of others – Syrians, Albanians, Tunisians, Somali, as well as his own countrymen. They slept on bedrolls on the floors of empty classrooms. The toilets were broken and there was one small kitchen to feed them all. The only good thing was the teacher, who came every day to give them Italian lessons and, because there was nothing else to do, Babacar worked hard. But it was from the teacher that he learned the truth about their position – that there could be no visa, no papers, no job. All that hardship had been for nothing. He was an illegal immigrant. There was even a rumour that they would all be sent back.

One day they were told that they were being taken to the hospital to have their chests x-rayed and be given some tests. He and another *Wolof*, Ahmed, packed some of their essential belongings into back-packs. The doctors took blood tests and shone lights into their eyes and down their throats. But for a time they were all left to their own devices. The guards who had come with them on the truck were sitting outside smoking. And then Ahmed had said, 'Let's go!' He was hoping to travel far north, to Milan, where he had a friend who would find them somewhere to sleep. Rome he'd been told, was full of Rumanians and Albanians who would rob you and kill you.

Babacar wasn't sure escape was the right course of action.

'What if they catch us?'

Ahmed shrugged. 'It can't be worse.'

But it was. The first night they slept in a shed that held stinking sheep, the next behind a wall in a stony field. They hitched a ride on a truck that put them down in a big town and then began jumping goods trains. Babacar remembers the fear and the hunger. They ate the discarded crusts of pizzas, raided the rubbish bins of restaurants and the piles of rotting fruit and vegetables behind the market. He wonders sometimes if Ahmed ever got to Milan and whether life would have been different there. Babacar had come here by accident. The train had pulled into a siding, as they often did at night, and he'd got off to have a crap in the vegetation at the edge of the track. The train had gone on without him. His friend Ahmed threw his back-pack off as the tail lights sped away in the darkness.

In the piazza the market stalls are being set up – it intrigues Babacar that the vans have lids on top that lift to reveal fan-shaped folds of metal and fabric that rotate and expand to provide a little roof to protect the stalls from sun and rain. Every trader has his or her routine – trestle tables, the neat plastic boxes of goods stacked in exact order, from the back of the van to the front. Coloured sweaters and dresses, shoes, kitchen implements and plastic buckets, Chinese watches, Indian bracelets, vegetables and table cloths, bed sheets and saucepans, flowers, cheese, salami and spit-roasted chicken – that's the stall that tempts Babacar the most – the smell of the birds turning on the spit, browning in olive oil and herbs. If he can sell enough to satisfy Selim, then perhaps he might be able to afford a wing, or a leg, perhaps one day a whole chicken.

Matteo at the Bar di Pietro sometimes gives him hot tea in the morning. In return Babacar keeps him supplied with cigarette lighters – Selim never misses one or two. But today Matteo is in the kitchen at the back having a conversation with his girlfriend – the beautiful Greek girl who works in the bar. They are arguing.

'You mustn't think of it,' he's saying.

'But what else can I do? It's the only sensible thing.'

'We'll manage. I'll talk to my father.'

'He won't like it Matteo.' The girl sounds as if she's crying.

Babacar turns and goes quietly out of the bar and across the piazza. In the pizzeria, Franco is in his kitchen. He has red eyes and his face is very flushed.

'Baba!' he calls. 'Come! We'll have a coffee together.'

Franco is raking the wood ash out of the oven. 'I try to keep it alight for market day, but last night it went out. Why is that do you think? Perhaps God just likes to annoy Franco? Perhaps he enjoys it?'

Babacar thinks perhaps it's not so much the will of Allah as the alcohol consumption of Franco and he says so, as politely as his limited Italian will allow.

'Ah,' Franco says, wiping his forehead with a hand covered in ash. 'But you are a tee-total *Musselman*, Baba! I am an Italian.'

He sits down at the table and mops his face with a sheet of kitchen roll. The heat coming from the brick interior of the oven is still strong.

'I light it for you,' Babacar says. He knows about these round, domed ovens. He stacks olive wood in the centre with some wood shavings and a shredded cardboard pizza box and leans in to ignite it with one of the gas stove lighters he had sold Franco last week. A flame blooms hopefully round the sticks, falters, and then with a little 'whoof' it leaps upwards.

'So, now I have earned my coffee,' Babacar says. He doesn't like to accept gifts. If people buy him drinks he always smiles and accepts so as not to cause offence, but it feels like begging. There are enough beggars in the piazza. The Tibetan, Taj, at least attempts to play music for his money, but there are others who carry plaques featuring hungry children they don't have, holding out a plastic pot and standing beside the tourists in the bars looking sad until they are irritated enough to put coins in the pot to make them go away. 'I will never be a beggar,' Babacar says firmly to himself. 'Never. I swear on my mother's honour.'

Babacar is walking along the main street to his lunch-time pitch near the car park. He's limping because his trainers have split. It's a problem. But maybe because it's market day there will be enough money to keep Selim happy and buy a pair of cheap sandals for himself. The weather is warmer now, so maybe he can make do without trainers.

The two elderly sisters are standing in the doorway of their shop, as usual, like spiders at the entrance to the web, trying to entice someone into it. The little one disappears inside when she sees him, but the taller one, Olimpia, smiles. Babacar stops. She likes to banter with him sometimes.

'Ha! Sister!' he always calls her this. 'You have something for my big feet?' He lifts up his left leg and the sole of the trainer obediently lolls its tongue at her. He laughs to show that he is not *sul serio*.

'Babacar! Don't tell me you can't get something from China for a better price than you can find here!' It is her usual joke with him.

He grins at her. 'You know they will fall apart in a week.'

Olimpia laughs. 'Like those ones.' She points at his feet. 'But you can't sell enough hats and cigarette lighters to afford a pair of mine – not in a whole summer!' It's a conversation they often have. But this morning she's looking down at his split trainers as if she's thinking. Then she says, 'Babacar, come inside.'

He leaves his pack at the door and follows her into the shop. There's a movement at the back and he glimpses the other sister slipping behind the curtain that he presumes leads to their living quarters.

Olimpia points at the upper shelves – a dizzy distance from the floor. 'If you can get some of those boxes down for me and find a pair of shoes on that shelf that will fit you – you can have them for nothing.'

'Madame. I get those shoes down for you, no problem, but is not necessary to give me something. *Nulla.*'

'Well, Babacar,' Olimpia is laughing again. 'You do not like to be given things for nothing, but then I don't like people to do things for me for nothing either. And maybe there won't be anything that will fit you? It is a risk for both of us.'

Babacar shrugs and grins reluctantly. 'Okay, madame. We have bargain.'

The ladder is old and shakes under his weight, but Babacar is able to clear the boxes from the shelf in a cloud of dust that fills his eyes and nose and makes him sneeze.

They are rich men's shoes, of fine leather, with thin soles that would never stand the miles he has to walk each day or the assault of mud and pebbles and rain. They are shoes for getting out of the car and going into a bar; shoes for restaurants and offices and dancing places. But in one of the boxes is a pair of what Olimpia says are golfing shoes. They are in black and cream leather, double stitched with good thick soles and a fringed tongue that folds over the laces at the front. They are half a size too big, but Babacar thinks he could maybe stuff the toes with newspaper.

'Take them,' Olimpia says. 'No one buys such things now.'

Babacar sits down to put them on, embarrassed by the holes in his socks, puzzled by the woman's sudden generosity. 'Why are you so good to me, madame?'

She looks down at him as if she can't understand the question and then she says, 'You are a Muslim, Babacar, aren't you?'

'Yes, madame.'

'And I think maybe people are unkind to you because of that?'

'You know about *Musselmen*, madame?'

'I knew someone, a long time ago.' Her mouth closes, and there's an expression in her eyes that tells Babacar she's not going to say any more.

He picks up his old pair of trainers.

'Here,' Olimpia holds out her hand. 'Give them to me! I'll put them in the bin.' She takes them from him, holding them away from her as if they were *ordure* and shuffles away into the back of the shop.

'Thank you madame. Thank you.' Babacar calls and goes out into the street to pick up his back-pack and the pyramid of hats and take up his position outside the Tabacchi.

There are two police officers approaching him from the side street. No hope of getting away. One is a girl, with long curly hair, slim and very pretty. He's seen her before.

'*Salve*, Babacar,' she says.

'*Salve!*' He forces himself to smile. He has found that this makes people less aggressive.

The man holds out his hand. 'Your papers.'

Babacar produces the tattered *Carta d'Identita* and the street-selling permit that Selim had given him. Fakes, but they are all the papers he possesses. The man looks at them for a long time.

The girl is admiring one of the bracelets. 'This is a very nice colour. I think my sister might like it.'

It's a dilemma for Babacar. If he offers it to her as a gift it might turn out to be a trap. But if she accepts? Is that what she wants – a little present? Babacar is cautious.

'I give you good price for your sister.'

The man is tapping the ragged piece of paper Babacar has given him. 'This is a permit for street-selling only,' he says.

The girl is twirling the bracelet around her hand.

'You can't sell from this,' the man points to the wheeled suitcase by Babacar's feet. 'This counts as a stall.'

Babacar keeps on smiling. 'A suitcase?'

'Yes, if it has wheels and you are selling from it, it is a stall.'

'How much?' the girl asks earnestly.

Babacar halves what he would normally ask. 'For you, five euros.' He's sweating.

'I must ask you to leave the piazza with the suitcase,' the man says. 'You must leave it somewhere else.'

'Okay.' That's all? Babacar is relieved.

'Three euros?' the girl asks, dangling the bracelet from her fingers.

Babacar gives her his biggest smile. 'For you, three.' His T-shirt is sticking to his back under the jacket. She puts three coins in his hand and slips the bracelet into her pocket. They walk with him as far as the Medici archway at the entrance to the piazza and then they turn right to go back to the Questura.

Franco is waving from the doorway of the pizzeria. Babacar checks to see that the *poliziotti* are out of sight and drags his suitcase back to the bar.

'The pigs fined you?' Franco asks.

'No, but they say I can't have my suitcase, so I have to find somewhere to leave it. That is the problem. How can a suitcase become a stall?'

'Don't talk to me about regulations!' Franco throws up his hands in a very Italian gesture. '*Porca puttana*! What we have to suffer in this bloody country.'

'But at least you have food and you have water.'

Franco laughs. 'It's crazy, Baba, that you live in a country where it never rains and you have to come here to sell umbrellas!' He gestures to the handles sticking out of the top of the suitcase. 'I tell you what, my friend, I will show you where you can leave your things.'

Babacar follows him round to the back of the pizzeria where the corner of the Michelangelo tower juts out into a small courtyard. Franco moves one of the big communal rubbish bins and there is a small wooden doorway in the wall behind it. Franco takes a key from his pocket and opens it. There are stone steps leading down into darkness.

'You need a torch,' Franco says, and Babacar takes one of the cigarette lighters out of his bundle, one of those with a key light on the end.

'There are tunnels down here that go right under the piazza – all the way up to La Rocca and the Porta da Pisa. Plenty of space! When you need to go in, you just ask me for the key.'

At the bottom of the steps there are racks of bottles and boxes of coffee and crisps. Everywhere there are bowls of grain with a strange, blue tinge. 'Those are for the rats,' Franco says. 'They eat this stuff and then . . .' he draws the side of his hand across his throat. '*Il povero topolino* – but they look much more cute when they are dead.'

Walking back later, to Selim's pick-up point at the station, Babacar begins to think about what he could do. He has the bicycle, and now he has a place to store his goods. If there was only somewhere to sleep, he could be independent. He could buy the goods from the same suppliers as Selim and keep all the money – perhaps one day he might have enough to send for N'gof and the children. Babacar feels happier than he has done for a long time. '*Allah wapert!*' he says aloud. God is good. It is a long time since he has heard it called from the mosque. He's not a religious man, an occasional attendee at Friday prayers, but the sound of the words can still make his heart leap in his chest. It happens all the time – a sound, a smell, the back of someone's head and a memory will jump out into the light and blind you just for a moment. '*Allah wapert!*' Summer is coming; he can sleep anywhere. Tomorrow he must talk to Brother Hermes – the Christian Arab – about how to get the proper papers.

4

The Messenger of the Gods

... 'Perhaps the only intention
of this unknowable earth, is to encourage
lovers towards ecstasy?'

Rilke, Duino Elegies, No 9

'What am I to do, Father?' Simona asks.

Hermes knows that she doesn't understand the distinction between monk and priest and that it's pointless to correct her. Only his fellow Franciscans call him 'brother' here.

The shutters are still open and the morning sun, already strong, casts the shadow of the lemon tree growing outside in the courtyard, across the marble tiles. It picks out the corner of the heavy wooden desk and frames one of Hermes' brown, rope sandals in a square of light. Simona is sitting with her back to the window.

'What am I to do?' She still has her hands clasped on her lap in an attitude of prayer, but her face is raised to him, lips trembling, and there's a tear trapped in the lashes of her left eye.

Hermes looks down at the floor, while he composes

a reply. It's easier to think without Simona's body in his line of vision. Every celibate has his demons. For some it's other men; for Hermes it's women. Not that Simona is particularly attractive, too full-bodied, her face broad and fleshy with a strong jaw. Her ample stomach and breasts strain at the cotton tunic that she's wearing. Please God, preserve me from the temptations of the flesh . . . Hermes lifts his head.

'You say Vittorio promised to leave you the house?'

'And the olive grove. He did. He said that he couldn't afford to pay me, but if I looked after him as if he was my own grandfather he would leave it all to me, because he doesn't have any children of his own. He said that he felt sorry for me – being left with the child.'

'Do you have any evidence of what he said?'

Simona nods. She opens her bag and pulls out a tattered piece of paper.

It's a handwritten testament – almost illegible and in very bad Italian. The old man probably speaks Liguro-Apuane, like most of the hill farmers here. But, as far as Hermes can tell, the document does say, *I will leave my house to Simona Viviani after my death, because she has been good to me*'. There's a spidery signature.

'You know he could revoke this at any time while he's still alive?'

The tear rolls down Simona's cheek. 'The old bastard! I've cooked for him and cleaned his house, and washed his sheets and his pants when he's pissed in them, for years and years . . .' She stops and lifts the edge of her tunic to mop her cheeks, revealing a line of bare flesh above the waistband of her trousers.

Hermes sighs. 'So, tell me again, how it happened.'

Italian is not his first language, or even his second. It's easy to miss something.

The girl composes herself. 'Last week, I went as usual to make his breakfast, after I put Paolo on the bus to the *Scuola Materna*, and this old woman was there. Well, I've seen her in the village because she and her sisters live in one of the houses just above Solaio where they have an olive grove. There are three of them and this one is the eldest. She opened the door and she said, "You can go away. You're not wanted here. I'm looking after him." And I couldn't get past her. I could hear Vittorio's voice in the room saying something and she turned her head and said something like "yes, yes, but don't disturb yourself, it's not important" and then she came outside and closed the door behind her and stood there with her arms folded and she told me, "You're not to come here again." I was so shocked I couldn't think of anything to say. "We all know what you are," she said, and she called me a money-grubbing whore and accused me of trying to steal an old man's property! "Well," she said, as though she was enjoying it, "we've found you out, and that's the end of your game. *Vaffanculo*, or I will make a *denuncia* to the police."'

Simona's voice is shaking. 'I went up again when I thought he might be alone and I waited until I saw the old witch leave. I knocked on the door, but it was locked and he wouldn't let me in.' She sniffs and mops her face with the edge of her tunic again. 'What am I to do Father? I thought God was looking after me and my little Paolo, but now it seems he doesn't care at all.'

'God cares for all of us, Simonetta,' Hermes says. He uses the diminutive of her name, as if she was still a child, as if to comfort her. Or perhaps to comfort himself, because the words feel like a lie. Since he came here he has begun to suspect that God doesn't care much for anyone. Where once his heart had blazed with faith, there is now only an empty space, as cold and heavy as marble. But these are his people and, whether God gives a toss or not, it's his duty to care for them. 'Leave it with me,' he says, standing up and letting his brown habit fall around him so that the coarse fabric rubs against his thighs. 'I'll go and see Vittorio and find out what's happening. It may be that something can be done.'

The girl also stands up, rather unsteadily. They say she drinks and she sometimes takes drugs, but it can't have been easy for her, widowed at twenty with a small child; her husband killed in the quarry by a ton of Carrara marble that swung the wrong way from the crane, pinning him to the wall. And on the whole Simona has coped – the child seems well fed and happy enough.

'How is Paolo?'

Simona smiles for the first time. 'He's fine. He likes the school and he comes home tired and is less trouble than he was.'

'Does he see his grandparents?'

'At the weekends, only one day. I still worry when I take him that maybe they won't let him come back.'

Hermes remembers the fight she'd had to keep Paolo after her husband's death when she'd been off her head with grief and substances and the grandparents had tried to take away the child. Simona is someone that life has not been kind to. If there is a God, then he is surely not interested in human affairs.

'Can I have the letter?' Hermes holds out his hand again. 'I'll look after it – make a copy. But I'd like to show it to *Avvocato* Baldacchini and find out what the law says.'

He folds the document carefully. 'Who else knows of this arrangement?'

'My landlady Orietta, and Franco and Stefania in the bar – I clean for them. And I told my brother in Querceta. He and his wife know.'

The afternoon sun is hot as Hermes climbs the track to Vittorio's holding. It's almost a kilometre from the place where the drivable road ends at a circle of brown earth. Hermes had parked the car beside a decrepit *Apè* that didn't look as if it had moved for a long time. Simona's devotion must have been very great for her to make this trek up from the village twice a day for the past four years. A greater devotion than his own.

Hermes stops to catch his breath and he turns towards the sea. From up here you can see out across the water to a line of islands shaded blue against the horizon. Capraia, Elba, Gorgona, and beyond them the dark spine of Corsica with a crown of cloud. It's very different to his native Lebanon – a place it seems impossible ever to go back to. Hermes is still conscious of a kind of hunger, for a language he does not have to struggle to understand the nuances of, for the shape of a landscape he can still see when he closes his eyes, for the village smell of fenugreek and dust and donkey-shit, for a name that belongs to him.

He had been born in the Bekaa Valley to a Maronite mother and a Druse father; Christian and Muslim, two utterly irreconcilable religions. A history of intolerance, massacre, mutilation and torture. He had not been called Hermes in those days, but Hassan. His father had been killed by a car bomb – or so he'd been told – it could have

67

been a lie. People simply vanished. Afterwards his mother had put Hermes into an orphanage, run by the Franciscans and the Poor Clares, and gone back to her family to beg forgiveness.

So Hermes had been brought up by the priests and the nuns. No one wanted a child of mixed blood and religion. But he remembers someone, maybe a grandfather, taking him to Baalbek once. He had stood, as a child of six or seven, in the Temple of Bacchus looking up at the great Roman pillars rising up towards the sky, and the mountains behind tipped with snow. They had seemed to shimmer, like a mirage or a waking dream, and he had felt his heart wrenched open inside him. That was why, later, when they asked him where he wanted to go, he had said 'Rome'. In Lebanon you either became a fighter, a refugee, or a priest of whatever religion had a mortgage on your soul. Hermes had no taste for inflicting suffering on others; it had remained simply to choose the manner of his leaving. A new life and a new name – and perhaps his new name is more appropriate than the one given to him at birth – Hermes the messenger, the god of transitions, of borders and boundaries. At least that is something that he knows.

Vittorio's door, as Simona had predicted, is locked. 'Piss off,' a voice says, when he bangs on it.

'It's me, Brother Hermes. Open the door Vittorio.'

There are shuffling steps and the sound of bolts being drawn back. The battered wooden door opens a crack and then is pulled back by an elderly man in shirtsleeves and sweat pants with a stripe down each leg. His red-rimmed eyes are bleary with sleep, but he has shaved.

'I need to talk to you,' Hermes says. The man

reluctantly shuffles to one side allowing him to enter. Hermes has to duck his head under the beam – these old houses were built for Tuscan dwarves.

The room is airless, stinking of farts and sweat and the swimming pool odour of bleach. Hermes takes a chair at the table and Vittorio sits down on the opposite side. Hermes produces the letter. 'Now,' he says, smoothing it out on the table. 'Tell me about this. And tell the truth – remember I am a priest.'

An expression that might be a leer, crosses Vittorio's face. A furtive shadow. He bobs his head towards the letter. 'Ah . . . that!'

'So, why have you gone back on your promise to Simona?'

'She was slovenly – didn't do things properly – and sometimes there were things missing – money even.'

The way he says the words sounds rehearsed and somehow too glib. But Hermes acknowledges that there could be some truth in it. Simona's character is not without blame. He has twice listened to her confession, though she probably hadn't realised who it was behind the grille.

'But she's looked after you for all these years, without payment, believing that you would make all your accounts straight after you died. You admit that?'

The old man bobs his head again. 'But she was no good!' he persists stubbornly. 'She doesn't deserve to have my house. Besides . . .'

'Besides what?'

'Now there is Angelina.' He begins to smile broadly. 'A magnificent woman.' His hands make a shape in the air in front of him. 'You know she prunes her own olive trees? And her legs – they are strong legs.'

'Ah . . . Is there something you should tell me

Vittorio?'

The old man's mouth is still curled in a lascivious smile. He lowers his voice to a whisper. 'God has sent her to me,' he says. 'Sometimes she lies beside me at night and, you know, she wears no knickers under her clothes.'

It's all Hermes can do not to laugh. Poor Simona – to be cheated out of a house by a seventy five year old woman who's prepared to take off her knickers for an old lecher like Vittorio.

'Is there any harm in it Father?' Vittorio's voice is wheedling. 'Sometimes she lets me touch her tits!'

He says it with such pride that Hermes has to lower his head to hide the involuntary smile. He forces his voice into a sterner tone. 'You know it is sinful to lie with a woman who is not your wife and harbour unclean thoughts?'

'I do. But it is also very nice. God has been kind to me, to give me a bit of pussy at my age. That slut Simona would never let me lay a finger on her butt . . .'

So that's it, Hermes thinks. Clever Angelina! Hermes knows all about the pleasures and temptations of the female form – the sheer delight of lying skin to skin, the scent of her, the silken pelt, the soft orifices, the glory that is so great it has to be God-given, but must be denied. How can he condemn Vittorio, who is not a priest vowed to celibacy, when his own sins are so much greater?

He gives Vittorio absolution and orders him to say his rosary. Then he tells him that in order to ready his soul for the journey to God that is surely not far off, he must put everything straight with Simona.

'You have not behaved as a good man should,' Hermes says sternly, standing in the doorway blocking the light.

Vittorio is making a strong effort to be contrite,

but there's a glint in his eyes that belies it.

They are all pagans up here, Hermes thinks. Throwbacks to the Etruscans. On the way to the car park, he walks past the little chapel on the hill above the village, which is no longer used because the ceiling has been damaged by an earth tremor and isn't safe. He had once been inside to see the black Madonna, with her dusky baby, her dress painted with flowers and herbs and a goat peeping from the folds of her skirt. It was supposed to be a lamb, officially, but Hermes knows a goat when he sees one.

In the refectory, the others have eaten and gone. Laura brings him a bowl of *cavolo nero* and a basket of bread from the kitchen.

'Wine?' she asks. Laura is an attractive woman in her forties; a widow who had loved her husband and now works for the priests because it's the only way she can make a living.

'Please.'

Laura places a tumbler full of red liquid in front of him and smiles. 'You'll need that I think.' She remains standing in front of the sideboard with her arms folded. She often stays to talk when Hermes eats alone. He finds her company comforting. Now she says, 'How was he?'

'Vittorio? Unrepentant. Difficult.'

'Mmmm. I knew him when he was younger.'

Hermes had forgotten that Laura had come from the same village. 'What was he like then?'

'A rogue. Drank too much grappa. He worked in the marble quarries, when his parents were alive. He was an only child and his mother treated him like a prince.

And no woman he ever looked at was good enough. His mother had wanted him to go for a priest, so they say, but he was refused by the seminary. Thanks be to God for that.' She crosses herself.

'Well, he's disinherited Simona in favour of Angelina Gallo. You know her?'

'That old cow! She's already buried two husbands.'

'She's warming Vittorio's bed now.'

'I doubt she'll get much out of him except for the money!' Laura gives an earthy laugh. 'Stupid fool! You get what you deserve. A pity for Simona though – she's not a bad girl. It's hard bringing up a child on your own.' She says it with feeling. Laura's children are grown up now, but Hermes guesses that she has known what it is to struggle.

Hermes mops his plate with the bread. 'What happened to Simona's family?'

'Oh, her father went off when she was a child – he was a drunk, and then her mother married again – a man *non simpatico*. Simona lived with an aunt for a while, until she got married herself. She was barely out of school. I hope you can get justice for her.'

Hermes pushes his plate away. 'I had a word with *Avvocato* Baldacchini on the way back. I have to take Simona to swear a statement. Apparently she should get a lump sum from the house to pay for her work, but she'll have to wait until Vittorio dies.'

'That won't be long if he's in the hands of Angelina Gallo!'

'I'm taking Simona along tomorrow to denounce him and sign the papers. Then it's up to the court. But I think they'll take her part. The letter is very clear.'

'*Speriamo!*' Laura raises her eyes to heaven as she

picks up the plate. She lifts the bottle to refill his glass, but Hermes shakes his head. He feels weary. The cabbage and beans are sitting heavily in his stomach and his head aches with the wine.

'Are there any messages?' he asks.

'Forgive me Brother, I forgot to say when you came in. Babacar, the Senegalese, was here but he will come back tomorrow. And the Tibetan man came about his dog again. I told him you were doing what you could. And I gave him some scraps from the kitchen.'

'You're a good woman Laura.' He would have liked to put his hand on her arm, a gesture of affection, to feel the gentle warmth that came from her, touch her quiet strength, but he restrains himself, forcing his hands, like lumps of meat, to sit obediently on the table.

She smiles quietly and picks up the glass. Her eyes dance a little, as if to say, 'I know what you are and what you want, but I don't judge you.' Earthly pleasures, Hermes thinks, we are all guilty.

But, as he walks through the cloisters to the church, a heretical thought occurs to him, as it does more insistently these days. What are we here for if not for that? Did God, if there is a god, create the earth simply as an experiment in human suffering? Or is it an accidental universe where men are simply one with the animals and driven by their endless pursuit of reproduction of the species? Is that our purpose on this earth? Because, if that is so, then his whole life has been for nothing. These are supposed to be his children, these troubled people, but it is terrible not to have fathered a child of his own blood.

Hermes kneels on the cold marble steps and murmurs the prayers he can say without even thinking the words. Above him, the wooden figure on the cross, a victim of extreme torture, hangs silently bleeding.

5

The Island of the Heart

Anastasia is fifty-four years old, but she's still beautiful.
Her bone structure has been inherited from a Georgian
mother. The wide cheekbones support dark Calabrian eyes
passed down by her father. The architecture of her face is
perfectly balanced by the soft hair piled up on top of her
head, held by a tortoiseshell pin that once belonged to her
mother. Anastasia is elegant, with the unconscious chic of
a Milanese, but most of her clothes are bought second
hand in the market. Today it is a sea-green suede jacket,
soft and thin as mouse fur.

In the morning she goes out to walk Fidel and get
an espresso. Anastasia knows that the local people call
her 'La Donna di Fidel' – Fidel's woman. He strolls beside
her, always slightly in front, squat, barrel-bodied with
a muscular chest and four short legs that take him only
where he wants to go. There's something of the bulldog
about him, but his tail whips up like a pointer, his muzzle is
long enough for a Great Dane, and his long, velvet ears are
constantly pricked for entertainment. Fidel will cock his
leg at anything, keeping a proprietorial eye on the woman
he trails on the leash.

'Why on earth did you choose a dog like that?'
her stepson had asked contemptuously. But Anastasia had

picked him out of the litter because she felt sorry for him; no one else wanted him. Fidel is a singularity.

The piazza is beginning to open for business. The two old women she thinks of as the 'shoe sisters' are unrolling the sun blinds over their shop window. One of them carries a chair outside and the other holds it while her sister climbs up with the long, metal arm to wind down the faded canvas.

'*Buon giorno.*' Anastasia always pauses to greet them.

'*Buon giorno signora. Com'è va?*' It is always the eldest who replies and she always uses the formal mode of address. The youngest says nothing.

Their bodies are small and crumpled and they have identical tonsures of curly hair dyed an improbable black. Like twins, they do everything together. There are rumours that they are the richest women in the street, but Anastasia doubts it. She recognises the little economies they practise. And she has never seen anyone buy a pair of shoes in the shop. Once she had gone in to see if she could find a comfortable pair of walking shoes. But they were all the wrong colour, or the wrong shape, or – more especially – the wrong price. When she had tried them all on and enquired the price of some, she apologised and tried to leave, but it had been hard to get out of the door. Would she not like to look at this pair? Could they not order that in a different size? Look, it was even possible to stretch this pair to fit? Eventually she had fled, never to return.

'Have you signed the petition yet?' The eldest sister asks.

'Against the Tibetan's dog?'

'Of course. That's no life for an animal. The poor

thing is starving.'

Anastasia nods. 'It's Clara's petition of course, although I don't like to agree with her on anything . . . because of the pigeons. They're such a nuisance – unhygienic and they put off the tourists. But I signed it yesterday.'

The older sister climbs down from the chair. 'Those birds! *Mamma mia*! I once asked her why she feeds them and do you know what she said?'

Anastasia waits.

'"Pigeons have babies too" – just that. Can you think of anything more ridiculous? "Pigeons have babies too".'

Which is more than I could ever do, Anastasia thinks. Gianluca would have liked to have had more children, but it was not to be. That was her big failure. She can still remember the pain and the bleeding – three or four times a year in the early days of her marriage. Then the examinations, the endless tests, the questions, the drugs. An empty womb. There was no explanation. Her body had simply refused to carry a child. So she had given her stepson Donato all the love that would have gone to her own. Now, it seems, for nothing, since he cares for her not at all.

Fidel is getting restless. It's time to move on. She says goodbye to Olimpia and Marina and walks off in the direction of the piazza.

There is never anyone in the Gallery before mid-day. Anastasia wonders why Carla bothers to open it so early, but suspects that it is to do with prestige and not money.

Sometimes the dealers come before lunch; Carla likes to have Anastasia there because she can speak so many different languages – Russian from her mother, English, French and Italian from her father and his friends. She can get by in German too at a pinch, though she doesn't like speaking it. This is her talent, something she's good at, sliding one word and its meaning past another. Sometimes one or other of the sculptors will ask her to translate a document for them; it's good money, but not frequent enough to pay the bills.

Carla isn't here today. Anastasia sits behind the desk with a woollen shawl over her legs to try to keep them warm. The temperature in the gallery is strictly controlled, in order to protect the paintings, and the spring sunshine hasn't yet lifted itself over the roof tops to penetrate the deep canyon of the street. Occasionally she gets up to walk around to keep the blood circulating.

The girl who comes in off the street is wearing the cargo pants and ragged T-shirt of a sculptor. Her hair is bound up in an Indian scarf and there are traces of marble dust in the folds. She goes round looking carefully at every piece, finally coming over to Anastasia's desk.

'Are you Carla Falcone?' she asks in careful Italian.

'No, sorry. She isn't here yet. I'm Anastasia. I just mind the gallery in the mornings. Can I help?'

'Oh. Probably not.' The girl looks disappointed. 'I just wondered how to get an exhibition here. Do you know?'

'You're working here?'

The girl smiles and holds out her hand. 'Rose Umber. I'm here on a scholarship from Canada, but I'm trying to find ways to stay on after the scholarship finishes.

I'm going to need to sell things.'

'Then you'll have to bring photographs and something about yourself for Carla. You have a catalogue?'

The girl shakes her head. She looks depressed. 'I hadn't thought of that. I can see I need to do some work before I start approaching galleries.' She pulls a face and then suddenly smiles at Anastasia. She seems a nice girl. 'Thanks for your help. Has the owner of the gallery got . . .' she hesitates, searching for the words, '*una carta?*'

'You mean *un billetto da visita?*' Anastasia smiles at the mistake and hands over one of Carla's glossy business cards. She watches the girl's youthful, optimistic progress towards the door.

At home Anastasia unlocks the post box in the loggia. A couple of fliers from the supermarket, the water bill, but still no cheque from Donato. Perhaps this is going to be one of those months when he forgets?

'Look after your mother,' Gianluca had said just before he died – before Anastasia found out that he had left everything to his son. The son that Anastasia had brought up as her own from the age of three. The son who called her mother because he couldn't remember his own. The appropriately named Donato had been a gift to her from her husband's first wife, dead from ovarian cancer at twenty four. It was possible that Gianluca, in the confusion of his last illness, had forgotten that Donato wasn't actually Anastasia's child. Thirty years of marriage – to be left nothing! Afterwards Donato had moved his wife and children into her home, squeezed Anastasia into the spare room above the garage and his wife had taken

79

over the kitchen and the garden and Donato had paid the bills and told Anastasia what she could and could not do. He had given her pocket money and his wife had priced her clothes. Dear God, if Gianluca could see!!

Luckily Anastasia had hung onto her parents' old apartment here, which was in her name. They had used it as a summer home when Gianluca was alive, and she was lucky there was still a trickle of royalties from her parents, lucky also to get the job in the gallery that paid cash on the black. Donato was supposed to send her a cheque for her 'maintenance' – a sum the lawyers had agreed – every month. But often it didn't arrive. 'Times are difficult,' Donato had said on the phone, 'the crisis . . . You can always come and live here if you can't manage.'

'I can manage,' Anastasia says to herself as she relocks the post box. But her fingers tremble as she folds the bill into her purse.

Anastasia thinks that the piazza is the most perfect work of art there is. The sky, gathering intensity towards evening, is the particular shade of blue of the Virgin's gown. The terracotta tower is reddening in the reflected sunset. Beside it, the marble of the Duomo is slightly yellow, like old teeth. The ochre colour of the buildings shade from pale yellow to deepest red, with every inflexion in between, and the windows are picked out by shutters of green and brown and sometimes a deep grey edged with blue.

'Why couldn't I have been a painter?' Anastasia says to Martin Soulby. She sighs, but he just laughs.

'If you were, you wouldn't want to paint this! Anyway, nobody knows how to paint these days. It's a lost art.' He flicks a long spill of ash into the tray and sucks on his roll-up to get it going again. 'So, what did your parents do?'

'They were writers. My mother was a Russian poet, from Georgia, but my father was Italian – a Calabrian. He wrote *Gialli* – thrillers – and did a lot of journalism to pay the bills. He spoke several languages fluently. At one time he was writing a column for the New York Times on Italian life.'

Martin takes a long gulp of his drink. 'My father worked in a saw mill.' He pauses to relight the tattered twist of paper and tobacco. 'Taught me to work with my hands. He wanted to apprentice me as a carpenter – didn't really understand when I went off to art school. He used to look shocked when I told him how much money I made – but he still didn't approve. It wasn't real work to him.'

'I didn't get any encouragement from my parents either,' Anastasia says. She can't remember getting any kind of direction from her mother or her father when it came to shaping her future, except for a vague sense of disapproval. 'For god's sake don't follow our example,' her father had once said. But for Anastasia it had always seemed natural to write. When she was young they had lived in Sardinia in a tiny shepherd's cottage in an olive grove overlooking the sea. There, her father had written his first two novels and her mother the collection of poetry she was most famous for, '*The Island of the Heart*'. Anastasia had translated it once, after her mother died, for some periodical in America that was doing a feature on her.

> *The island of the heart*
> *to which you voyage*
> *is forever at a distance*

just over the horizon
a shadow between sea and sky
between dream and reality. . .

'My parents lived in another world,' Anastasia says to Martin. 'And they shut me out – maybe they were just careless, or maybe it was deliberate. But it was painful.'

She can remember being eight or nine, at school in Sardinia, before they moved to the mainland. Anastasia had written a poem and everyone thought it was marvellous. She had brought it home, trembling with anticipation, fear and excitement, and showed it to her mother, who was sitting at her desk, as she always was in the afternoons. She had paused, slid her glasses down her nose for a moment, glanced at the page her daughter was holding up and said *'Brava, cara, brava,'* before turning back to the typewriter.

Anastasia had stood there, holding the paper, waiting, but her mother didn't look at her again, just kept pecking at the keyboard with her fingers, copying something from the notebook on the table beside her.

'They don't mean to be cruel,' Martin says. 'But they are.' He's rolling another cigarette and pauses to put it in his mouth and flick the lighter. At the third attempt a little flame appears and he draws deeply on the cigarette. 'God knows what we've done to our own kids.'

Has she been a good mother? Anastasia has certainly tried. 'I stayed at home to give my stepson a secure childhood, rather than get a job, and I listened to the priests. I wasn't going to be like my parents, two laughing, fornicating pagans.' She takes a sip of her wine. 'But now I wonder. He doesn't treat me very well, so perhaps I got it wrong.'

The young Greek girl is collecting the dirty glasses

from neighbouring tables. 'Now there is a girl who is not being treated well,' Martin says, nodding his head towards her.

Pia sees the nod and comes over, taking out her pad. 'You want to order?' Today she is without her usual smile.

'Why not?' Martin says. 'Another negroni for me. Anastasia?'

'A glass of water.'

Martin pulls a face. 'You're going tee-total?'

Anastasia waits until Pia has gone. 'Have you seen the price of the drinks here? They used to be reasonable.'

'Ah, but now the town is changing – it's not a "city of art" any more, it's becoming a holiday destination for the rich. Prices are going up everywhere and all the little studios are being turned into restaurants and designer clothes shops.'

It's true Anastasia thinks. None of the shops sell anything useful.

When Pia brings the drinks back, she hovers for a moment longer than necessary.

'How's things?' Martin asks.

'Okay.' Pia looks nervous. Then she asks suddenly, 'Do you know anyone who has a room they would rent out – not expensive. Just temporary?'

Martin shrugs. 'I'll ask around – there are always rooms going with people in the studio. Fallen out with Matteo?' He jokes, but Pia looks almost ready to cry.

The girl has put on weight recently – Anastasia glances at her profile and wonders. But before she can say anything, there's a disturbance at the next table, where two middle-aged tourists are drinking prosecco in tall glasses with little baskets of crisps and olives on the side. They're absorbed in each other and haven't been taking any notice of the pigeons until two or three of them swoop down on the table scattering crisps and feathers and spilling one of the glasses over into the lap of the woman. She screams as the birds graze her hair in their clattering flight.

Enzo rushes out, loud and red with anger. He is apologising to the couple in halting French. Free drinks are promised – the cleaning bill for a dress. Pia is ordered to bring another glass of prosecco. Turning to Anastasia, Enzo lets fly in vigorous Italian.

'That mad woman – she ought to be locked up – I've made a *denuncia* – more than once – but what do they do? Perhaps they're afraid of the old witch. *Porca misere!* How am I to make a business here with these birds everywhere?'

'He poisons them,' Anastasia tells Martin when Enzo has gone back inside. 'Feeds them poisoned grain early in the morning. You can't blame him, but it's nasty.'

The two sisters are walking across the piazza towards the bar, a little unsteadily, as if they've already had too much to drink, though Anastasia knows they rarely take anything more alcoholic than a *café corretto*.

'Oh, god!' Martin has also seen them. 'Here come the retards.'

'Why do you call them that? It's unkind.'

Martin laughs. 'They look like dwarves. That's Enzo's nickname for them, "*I nani*". And have you ever heard the smallest one say anything?'

'You're a bit of a bastard, Martin. Do you know that?' Particularly after a few drinks.

'Of course. But I like to tell things how they are. Can't stand all this politically correct mush.'

'You shouldn't make fun of the sisters though.

Their lives have been quite tragic.'

Martin raises one eyebrow, waiting for her to go on.

'They say that after the war, when there were a lot of refugees and displaced people here, one of the sisters had a lover who was not approved of in the village. And so they dragged him out of his house and beat him to death. Then they buried his body in a hole like a dog. Apparently someone had put out a rumour that he had raped one of the girls. But it wasn't true.'

'Where did you get that story?'

'Nonna told me. She knows everything about everyone round here.'

Martin looks unimpressed. 'You know what really gets to me?'

Anastasia looks at him, waiting.

'The way they still remember the fucking war. Christ! You'd think they'd have forgotten about it by now, but they're still a load of fascists or communists depending on which bar you drink in.'

'I try to stay out of politics here. It's too complicated.'

Anastasia gets up to go – she takes out her purse and opens the compartment where she keeps the loose change – her drinking money – and begins to pile the coins up beside her glass.

'Oh, leave it!' Martin says, waving his hand. 'I'll get them.'

It pains Anastasia to let him, but she manages a smile and a little nod of appreciation. He blows her a noisy kiss.

He's an asshole, Anastasia acknowledges, but she's known him for years, from the time he first came here as a successful sculptor casting bronze and paying the *artigiani* to cut marble for him. Now, he doesn't do much, or so she hears; drinking the profits he made in the fat years. And she has heard that he still owes Shira at the Studio Bertolozzi for the last lot of marble. So she will let him make the grand gesture in the bar.

Anastasia is lying awake wondering what she can sell to pay the property tax. Now that the government have raised the IMU to help bail out the bankers, it's almost as expensive to own property as to rent it. 'There's no such thing as a free apartment,' Anastasia says to herself in the dark. Perhaps she could steel herself to stay with her son for July and August and rent her apartment out to tourists. You could make seven hundred and fifty euros a week in the high season. Could she bear it? Or perhaps she could sell something. There are still a couple of paintings that her parents had bought when they had money and things were going well. Anastasia remembers those convivial evenings in the bar – groups of artists and writers all drinking together and then some of them would come back to the apartment and her mother would cook. The rooms seem very empty now. Cold and silent.

But at that moment the doorbell rings, loudly and persistently. Who can it be, so late? It rings again. Anastasia speaks nervously into the entry phone.

'Who's there?'

'It's the police. Open up!'

The police? Has something happened to Donato? 'One moment.' Anastasia goes into the sitting room and peers through the shutters. There are two men in the uniform of the *Polizia Communale* standing outside the door.

Quickly she puts on a coat over her nightdress and a pair of boots, calls Fidel from his basket and goes downstairs.

When she opens the door she sees that they are drunk. 'What do you want?'

'We have brought your census forms.'

'So late?'

'Ah, yes, *ci scusi signora*, we have been partying a little along the way. People are very kind to invite us in. Have you got some grappa? A little *digestivo* perhaps?'

'Absolutely not.' Anastasia is shaking. Fidel is growling and she tightens her grip on his collar. The men step back as the dog bares his teeth and Anastasia takes the opportunity to snatch the papers one of the policemen is holding out and slam the door in their faces.

One of them laughs and the other says, 'That is not kind. We thought you might be kind to us.'

'Go away, or I will make a *denuncia*.' Fidel is barking.

There is a silence on the other side of the door. A suppressed giggle. Anastasia goes back upstairs. Her hands are still trembling as she puts the papers on the table and switches on the kettle. She pats Fidel and runs her hand over his long, soft ears. 'Good dog. Beautiful dog.' What kind of country is it when you can't trust even the police?

Pia looks very uncomfortable sitting at the kitchen table.

'It would be pleasant to have some company,' Anastasia says. She's boiling the water to make a *tisane*. 'But of course the room isn't very big. It was mine, when I was a child, you know.'

'It would only be for a little while – until I can sort myself out – I can't stay at the bar any longer.'

87

'Forgive my being frank, but are you pregnant?'

Pia nods and begins to weep, her head down towards her lap. Anastasia moves behind her and puts her hands on the girl's shoulders.

'Matteo's?' she asks.

'Yes.'

'And will he not look after you?'

'His father says I'm a whore and a slut and I have to leave. Matteo won't say anything because he depends on his father for the job and the money. I'm afraid of Enzo – he isn't safe. The way he looks at me sometimes . . .'

'You're right. It will be best to leave for a while until Matteo has come to his senses. He's not a bad boy you know – but he's also afraid of his father. With reason. You know Enzo used to play tapes of Mussolini's speeches late at night when he was drunk?' Anastasia shrugs. 'Maybe he still does.'

'Matteo said something about it – I thought he was joking.'

'Enzo's wife told me.'

Pia looks shocked.

'But what are you going to do if Matteo does nothing? Can you go home to your parents in Greece?'

Pia shakes her head. 'There's no work in Greece now. My parents are old – they need me to send money.'

'What will you do if you don't work in the bar?'

'I trained in fashion design in Athens you know, that's why I came here – what I wanted to do. Maybe I can find something – make clothes for people.'

Anastasia doesn't think there's a snowflake's chance in hell of a *straniera* getting a job in the fashion business here except as a shop assistant. If Pia hasn't managed in the eighteen months she's already been here, she isn't going to now, four or five months pregnant. But Anastasia doesn't say that.

'Come here for a couple of months,' she says. 'Just until things settle down. Have you money for the rent?'

'Yes. I have some savings and Matteo says he'll give me money for the baby.'

'Good. And I have an idea.'

'Oh?'

'I'm going to write to Matteo's mother. Have you ever met Mari-Elena?'

Pia shakes her head.

'We were friends once – our husbands were both businessmen and we used to go out together when we were here during the summer months. Once she even came up to Milan and stayed with me. After Enzo divorced her she went back to Turin with her daughters to be near her family. She is very nice and I think she might help you.'

'I don't want to make trouble for people.'

'Oh, Pia! You have enough trouble yourself without worrying about what it does to others. It's Matteo's trouble too, you know, and his family must shoulder some of it.' She pauses. 'Besides, this might be a good time. Enzo is standing for *Sindaco* and he won't want any bad publicity.'

After Pia has gone, Anastasia takes out her address book and the writing case. She spends some time hunting for a pen that will work. It's a long time since she's written anything but an email. When she thinks about Pia and the hapless Matteo she feels very angry. Maybe it would be better to do nothing, after all – what use is such a spineless boy to a girl like Pia. But is it his fault that he's never been allowed to stand on his own feet? Perhaps this could be the making of him. Anastasia sighs.

'My dear Mari-Elena,' she begins . . .

6

Rose Umber

The June sunlight, reflecting from the pale ochre walls, fills the room with light the colour of butter. Rose feels the pleasure of it spreading through her body from the moment she opens her eyes. Pierluigi is still dozing beside her, replete with sex, a long lunch in the Co-operativo, and the kind of satisfaction that comes from being comfortable in one's own skin.

Rose lies quietly, watching the light ripple across the ceiling as the muslin curtains billow restlessly in the afternoon breeze. There's a faint shadow of unease underneath the feeling of well-being, but it seems to be always like that here – surges of delight with an undertow of anxiety.

Pierluigi stirs and opens his eyes. 'Hello!' he says and rolls towards her to put his arm across her body in a gesture of possession. His skin is dark from working outside naked to the waist – almost as black as the Senegalese street traders – while hers is as pale as the bed sheets. He had laughed about it, the first time. Her North American, indoor look.

'I thought the sun shone in America?' he had said, running a finger down her breast bone with a touch that made her shiver.

'Not where I come from. I'm Canadian, not American. And it's always raining on Vancouver Island.' Her home is in Port Hardy, as far north as you can go and, though summers are dry, it rains constantly from October through to March.

Rose had tried to describe to Pierluigi the grey shawls of rain dragged in by the clouds off the Pacific ocean – the sense of living on the edge of such vast emptiness, but it was impossible. Here, everything is small – even the sea. The Mediterranean is scarcely a pond in comparison; the marble mountains mere hillocks compared to the mighty Pacific Ranges. But it's this smallness Rose likes – it has a human scale

Rose. She rolls the word around her head. It's the name everyone here knows her by – the one she has chosen for herself. Her mother had said – why do you want to change your name? Aggrieved. But whoever heard of a sculptor called Susan Zukermeier? Most people couldn't even spell it. Rose has never felt like a Susan in her life. Not even Sue and definitely not Suzy. But Rose Umber . . .

Rose-umber is a colour, but it's difficult to describe. It's the exact shade the low, afternoon sun paints on the walls of the buildings around the piazza. Warm, earthy, delicately pink and grey-brown like the pelagic limestone that comes from Umbria, shadowy with fossilised life forms, rich in iron-oxide, glowing like a sunset when polished. Rose had learned about it when she first came here and began to study marble.

It's after four o'clock when Rose gets back to the studio. Shira's office door is open and Rose can see her scowling with disapproval as she lifts her head to see who is going past. She knows what I've been doing, Rose thinks and feels a flush of shame. But why should she feel ashamed of taking a couple of hours off after lunch? Why should she feel guilty about going to bed with the attractive *artigiano* provided by the studio? This is the twenty-first century. She's a free woman. But it's as though Shira has read the small print on Rose's scholarship documents – as though she's tapped into the psychology of the grave-faced committee who had awarded it back in Vancouver. What an opportunity – six months in an Italian marble studio, all expenses paid – the assistance of an experienced technician – not a moment must be wasted! Rose must lap it up greedily – devour every second before she goes back to rainy, dull Port Hardy.

Rose picks up her chisel and turns on the compressor. Shira has come to the door and is watching her. Rose focusses on the pale shape on the stand in front of her, concentrates on the lines and curves – tries to identify where she needs to shave a fraction of a centimetre, which of the lines needs to be sharpened. Only one month left. Rose feels sick. One month!

Pierluigi strolls in a few moments later, looking very pleased with himself. Shira gives him the same frown, but turns round and goes back into her office. Today, Pierluigi is working with two women from Germany who've come to learn how to sculpt marble. Rose finds them irritating – they talk constantly, discussing dress shops and restaurants and asking interminable questions about the right tools to use. They know nothing. They're tourist sculptors – hobby artists – older women with rich ex-husbands who are trying to find some creativity in their lives.

Rose has seen the end results – small polished marble objects without any form or meaning – a nice shape they can put on a table in their homes in Munich or Berlin and call themselves sculptors. Shira seems to be taking on a lot of them at the moment – driven by the need to make money to keep the studio going during the recession. Rose watches Pierluigi helping one of them with the pointing device, his hand resting lightly on her shoulder showing her how to line it up and she's surprised by a spasm of something she can only describe as jealousy. It's a feeling she can't allow. That was their agreement – no strings – absolutely no strings. She is only here until the end of July.

At six o'clock Trine comes across the yard. She's covered in black dust and takes the air line to blow it out of her overalls and her hair. She sluices her face and her arms under the tap. Trine's working with Belgian Black and the dust gets everywhere.

'Are you walking down to the piazza?' she asks. Her English has a lovely Scandanavian lilt that Rose finds very attractive.

She locks her tools in the cupboard and they go out of the gate together, with just a little smile and a wave to Pierluigi.

The street is narrow, like a canyon – the evening sun just catching the windows of the third floor apartments. But down on the pavement it's cool. The shops are opening for the evening – restaurants putting out the tables and chairs – at the Enoteca they are shaking out the table cloths and placing the big jars for the candles in the centre. There's a sense of expectancy – like a theatre waiting for the curtain to go up and the audience to arrive. It gives Rose a strange feeling in her chest, as if she's been holding her breath too long. How can I leave all this? she thinks.

'How long are you here for?' Trine asks, as if she

knows what's on Rose's mind.

'I've only got a month left, but I can't bear to go.'

Trine laughs. 'You're hooked. Like the rest of us. Can't you just stay on? Rent another place? There are plenty of empty studios.'

'No money,' Rose says. 'I've been here on a scholarship grant. I've got a little bit saved, but not enough. I was hoping to sell something, but it hasn't happened.' When she had come, the first week, everyone had told her that the Studio Bertolozzi was a really good place to get noticed; Bottero and Miteraj worked in the foundry next door, so all the visiting art dealers wandered through. And a Very Famous Sculptor, whose name must never be mentioned, was having some stuff done – there was a secret shed at the bottom of the marble yard, where no one was allowed to go except the *artigiani* who were working on the sculpture. No one was supposed to know, but everybody did. Rose sighs. So far none of the visiting dealers has given her little abstract marble a second glance.

Martin Soulby, the big English sculptor whose reputation had so impressed her when she arrived here, is sitting in the Bar di Pietro. He had taken an interest in her at that first meeting – asked about her work.

'Ah, you're Canadian!' he had said.

'How do you know? Everyone thinks I'm American.'

'It's the way you say "About" – the way you shape those vowels. I had a big exhibition once in Montreal – there's a sculpture of mine outside the Bank of Canada. Maybe you've seen it?' He sounded hopeful.

Rose had shaken her head, 'Sorry. I've only been to Montreal once – it's a big country.' And after that he seemed to lose interest.

Rose heads automatically for the Bar di Pietro, but Trine hangs back. 'Can we go to Franco's instead – do you mind?'

Rose shrugs – 'No problem!' but she's puzzled.

'It's Nonna,' Trine says. 'You know? The midwife! She's there – sitting at the back.'

'You don't like her?'

'It's not that. Look, let's get a drink.'

Stefania takes their order and comes back with a bowl of potato chips and another of olives.

Trine seems unhappy. 'It's an old story – a bit sad. I used to have a relationship with her son – a lovely guy, but a bit up and down. You know? He was absolutely obsessed with me and wanted to get married, have kids – but I got a bit scared, broke it off and went back to Copenhagen. And then he followed me.'

'What happened?'

'I suppose I was a bit cruel to him – I wasn't ready for a relationship – I felt a bit – crowded – you know?'

Rose nods.

'So, I let him stay a little bit – which was wrong – and then it all got too much and I told him to go away.'

'And?'

'He took an overdose in my apartment while I was doing a symposium in Sweden – he still had a key. And then the police came and they made contact with his mother and everything, but she doesn't believe that he's dead. Won't believe it. Every time she sees me she asks where he is and when he's coming back. Maybe she's senile. But I hate it!'

Rose thinks it must be horrible to have someone so obsessed with you, though she can't see that ever happening with Pierluigi. He knows she doesn't want a settled relationship. There's too much life still to be lived. No strings.

The Albanian boys are sitting at the next table drinking lemon sodas. The youngest one smiles at her. Zamir. He has nice eyes and Rose likes the way his hair curls over his forehead.

Pierluigi is frowning as he walks towards them across the piazza. Rose isn't sure whether this is because she's sitting with Trine, or because he's seen her smiling at Zamir. Pierluigi always seems wary of Trine – some subtle personality clash Rose can't read. Rose also knows that he thinks illegal immigrants are a waste of space.

'They cost us,' he'd said once when she'd expressed sympathy, 'but they don't contribute.'

'I think they do.' Rose had felt angry on their behalf. 'They work really hard. Everyone says so. And it's not as if they take housing away from anyone. Those caravans Father Hermes got them are really rough.'

'I don't like them,' Pierluigi had said, unmoved.

It had shaken Rose a little, to find that Pierluigi – otherwise a nice, caring sort of guy – was so hostile towards the refugees.

Rose looks up from her spritz and sees Zamir smiling at her, and then he looks away and blushes. Pierluigi is looking at her too, but in a challenging kind of way that doesn't bode well for the evening.

'Are going for a pizza tonight?' Trine asks. 'I'm way too tired to cook. That bloody Belgian Black is so hard to polish!'

Pierluigi grins. 'You should get me to do some of it. I did warn you it would be difficult.'

'I can't afford your prices. If it was a commission . . .' Trine leaves it hanging. 'Anyway. Pizza anyone?'

Rose mentally counts the euros in her purse and nods.

'If Franco's sober, I will,' Pierluigi says. 'If he's drunk it's a risk. I don't know how he stays in business.'

'It's so bloody sad,' Trine pulls a face. 'Why can't someone talk sense into him? He'll lose Stefania if he carries on like this.'

'His mother died when he was four years old and he was brought up by the Jesuits.' Pierluigi takes a long pull from his beer. 'I don't think you ever recover from something like that.'

The Albanian boys are leaving. Zamir is hovering behind Rose's chair and obviously wants to say something.

Trine says, 'Hi Zamir. You okay?'

He blushes again, but manages to say, 'We have music later. At the *ruolotte*. If you want . . . you come?'

It's the first time Rose has ever heard him speak. She smiles up at him. 'I'd love to. It sounds great.'

'I'm not sure I've got the energy.' Trine yawns.

Pierluigi doesn't look pleased. 'You can't go on your own,' he says to Rose. 'But I've got to be at the Studio early tomorrow to get some work in before it closes for the demonstration.'

'Oh, I'd forgotten about that.' But live music seems too good an opportunity to miss. 'I'm only here for a few more weeks.' She looks at Pierluigi's disapproving expression and nods acceptance to Zamir.

Rose wakes with the sun on her face. Her skin is burning. Hadn't she closed the shutters last night? Her head feels heavy on the pillow. It's an effort to turn over and face the other way. She tries to swallow, but her mouth is dry. Something tells her that it's late. Another black mark in Shira's books. Rose is beginning to worry that her report back to the funding committee isn't going to be favourable. 'Rose Umber doesn't take her vocation seriously enough.' That's what Shira will say.

Rose opens her eyes – the light is blinding. She lifts her lids again, cautiously. The bed clothes are folded back on the other side of the bed, the pillow skewed, but there's no one there. She slides a hand over. The sheets are cold.

She tries to remember who had come home with her last night. Pierluigi? No. Rose has a flash of remembered conversation. An argument. He'd accused her of flirting – what a horrible expression – with one of the Albanian boys. She touches the pillow, puzzled by a faint dark powder dusted over the linen. Belgian Black. Rose's stomach feels queasy. The bathroom seems a long way away – an expedition – a giddy ascent and descent and then the endless traverse across the slippery marble, with nothing to hold on to, before the open doorway to the cool, blessed darkness of the *bagno*.

It's too late to do any work, but Rose is in time for the demonstration. At the studio they're handing out hats made from newspaper – the kind the old *artigiani* used to wear to keep the dust out of their hair. Each workman had his own style.

Shira has made placards to carry, with names painted on them in big black letters. The old man standing next to Rose, wheezing a little, tells her that they are the names of all the studios that have closed in the last ten years.

'People don't want marble fountains in their

gardens, or marble coffee tables for their sitting rooms – they go to Ikea.' He spits the word out with contempt.

'No, Luca,' the man standing beside him says. 'It's because the churches are closing. They don't buy Madonnas and pietàs and fonts any more. No one wants what we do – not even God!'

Rose's Italian is good enough, just, to understand the substance of what they say, but not enough to make a contribution to the conversation. There is no money in the world any more for sculptures, for works of art, things of beauty. Only the super-rich can afford them and they – Rose is surprised how strongly she feels about this – they have no taste.

The jewelled angel in the locked shed at the bottom of the yard will be bought by a billionaire in Dubai or Surinam, but who will buy the quiet thing that is taking shape under her own hands, with its flowing lines and its relationship to the Golden Section – something that can touch the soul with its harmony and balance? It is the nearest Rose has ever come to the perfect shape she had seen in her mind when she first approached the marble.

The crowd at the gate is beginning to form into a line, and the band has arrived – the little orchestra from the village – formed from the quarry workers and the *artigiani* who live up there. Many of them are young men, which surprises Rose, since it seems such an old-fashioned thing to do.

The two old men are still arguing. 'Look at them, Luca!' The old man is saying. 'There's more than a thousand years of skill and tradition behind us – but there are no jobs for the young people any more.' He turns to Rose. 'Isn't that what we are marching for?'

One of the holiday sculptors is arguing with Shira

because she's closing the studio for the demonstration and the woman is asking if there will be money back in lieu of the time wasted.

'We have paid to come here,' the woman is saying, 'not to sit in the piazza and watch everyone parading around in fancy dress.' She waves a hand towards them in their overalls and paper hats.

Rose can't keep quiet. 'If we don't go out and demonstrate, perhaps this studio too will be closed and then there will be nowhere for you to come next year. You should be marching with us. Here. Have my hat! I can get another.'

Shira is looking at Rose in surprise, but she isn't angry. There's something like approval in her eyes. She turns round suddenly and walks firmly to the gate. 'Everybody out!' she shouts and flicks the compressor switch to OFF.

The woman ignores Rose's piece of folded newspaper and walks over to pick up her bag from the bench.

'Our great-great-grandfathers many times removed, worked for Michelangelo,' the old man says as they move off through the gate. 'That knowledge is in my hands and the hands of my brother Luca. But it will die with us if we don't pass it on. Doesn't that make you sad?'

'Very sad,' Rose says. She holds her placard higher – it reads Studio Apuano – named for the marble mountains rising above the town, but evidently not as long lasting. Rose doesn't know exactly why she is drawn to sculpture, but perhaps it's because she loves the permanence of stone – a rock is exactly that – you'll find it where you left it when you come back – it won't disappear in the night while you're asleep.

'I hope you don't mind that I didn't wake you

when I left this morning?' Trine says as they parade past the Academy on their way down to the piazza. 'You were really out of it last night.'

'It was you?'

'Yes. I brought you home and then I was too tired to walk all the way back to my flat.'

'I drank too much,' Rose says. 'Sorry.'

'The Albanian boys were scandalised.' Trine has very white, even teeth when she smiles. 'They don't drink and they think a woman drunk is just the worst thing in the world.'

'I was past caring.'

'I know. What's the problem?'

Rose sighs. 'There's so little time left . . . I really don't want to go back to Canada.'

'So, what are you going to do?'

'I want to stay.' At that moment, Rose has never wanted anything more in her entire twenty-four years of life. She wants to belong here; to become part of the tradition. 'But it's so difficult. I've saved some of my scholarship money, but not enough to rent an apartment and pay studio fees.'

'There are ways.' Trine says. She leans over and touches the arm of the old man on Rose's other side. 'Giorgio!' Shouting above the music that is bouncing off the walls of the street. 'Giorgio!' switching into Italian - 'Do you know a studio – cheap – where this girl could work?'

'Marcone,' he shouts back. 'You remember Marcone? He has some space in the yard and he might take someone. She can ask.'

Trine turns to Rose. 'He makes bathroom fittings and floor tiles for wealthy Milanese. He has all the

102

machines.'

'Where?'

'Just out of town, near the Aurelia, round the back of the Conad supermarket. It's no distance on a bike.'

To go or stay? She's drinking too much again, but after her fourth red wine, Rose no longer feels the panic rising up in her chest whenever she asks the question. Such a risk. No! Not a risk, something inside her says. This is an adventure. If you don't do it, if you go home, you'll regret it to the end of your life. But if you sell your air ticket, the other voice argues, there will be no money to buy a new one in a few months time if things don't work out. Don't be an idiot!

But there's hope, the first voice insists. Thea from the *comune* had looked at her work yesterday and asked if she was going to be here at Christmas, because there was going to be an exhibition – a small show for the people who were working here. It might not happen, but if Rose isn't here, it can't. There are only four more weeks. Her mother is already emailing to say that she has Rose's room ready and what time is the plane arriving?

And then Trine says, 'I've been thinking. I've got to go back to Denmark next week for the summer – I'm doing a symposium and then I've got some work in Copenhagen. You could house-sit my apartment for two or three months.'

'Could I?'

'You want to see? It's very small. Old. I got it years ago when I first came. I had a lot of money from a big commission from some Russian guy. You wouldn't have to pay anything for rent, so long as you pay the bills and look after the place. Come and have a look.'

Trine's flat is on the fourth floor of one of the nineteenth century palazzos off the main street just as the town begins to struggle uphill towards the old walls, but the entrance is just round the corner from the big four star hotel and there's a view of the Duomo roof and the bell tower from the bathroom window.

There's no bath – just an expanse of grubby tiling with a rusty shower over the loo and a small hand basin. The living room is a dark, echoing space, with antique furniture too big for the room. Rose notices a very uncomfortable looking wooden settle, a carved cupboard with worm-eaten doors and a display shelf stacked with chipped Majolica. There's no kitchen, only a stone sink and gas rings in a corner with a small fridge. The bedroom is at the back overlooking a central courtyard at the bottom of a narrow funnel of light that goes up from the ground floor to the roof. The window is screened from the pigeons with green mesh that shrouds the glass and allows a kind of underwater light into the room. No air-conditioning. A rather precarious wooden fan with brass fittings is screwed to the ceiling.

'It's very basic,' Trine apologises. 'But it's somewhere to sleep and you don't have to spend a lot of time in it. Let me know quickly though, won't you?'

Franco's sitting on the back step of the Pizzeria, reading a comic.

'What's that?' Rose asks.

'*Vernacoliere*. Not for the eyes of a lady.'

'Oh, come on Franco. That's so old-fashioned!'

He grins and shows her the page he's looking at.

'Berlusconi being suffocated by a giant pussy. It is the dream of many Italians.'

'So why do they vote for him?'

Franco shrugs. 'Most Italian men would like to be Berlusconi – the money, the women, the power.'

'And you?'

'Why not?' For a moment he seems serious and then he laughs. 'But he is a crazy man. *Pazzo*! The whole of Italy is in the hands of a lunatic.'

'So, should I stay in this crazy country Franco?'

He looks up at her, trying to hold his gaze steady. '*Sul serio?*'

'Seriously. I've been offered the loan of an apartment and if I'm very careful, I can just about manage.'

Franco takes out another cigarette and lights it with one of Babacar's lighters, decorated with a naked woman. 'You must do what you want – what you really want. Otherwise afterwards you will think about what might have happened and regret it.'

'But it's such a risk Franco. If I sell my return ticket and it doesn't work out, I'll have to beg my parents for the money to go back and they'll never let me forget it.'

'Never, never refuse an adventure.' Franco waves the cigarette in the air. 'Think of Mick Jagger. If he had led a sensible life and done what his parents wanted him to do, no one would know his name!'

'Anyway,' Franco says, after another long suck on his cigarette. 'You will be okay. And if you are starving . . .' he gives her one of his huge grins, 'I will feed you a pizza.'

'That's a promise?'

He holds up his hand to high-five her. 'A

promise.'

7

The Big Joker

It's unusual to have such a wind in high summer. A light breeze from the sea in the evening perhaps, or a brief squall to accompany a thunderstorm, and sometimes overnight an air current from the Sahara that coats everything with thick, red dust. But this wind is not like that. It springs up around two o'clock, pouring down from the mountains out of a clear blue sky – a wall of air, stripping the blossoms from the Oleanders, swirling newspapers and paper napkins from the tables around the piazza and tugging the parasols so that they strain and billow like sails in a gale and Franco has to run out and furl them, tying them with cord to stop them flapping at the customers' elbows.

On the promenade, it blows the spray from the waves back out to sea, making old ladies walk bent down towards the ground to avoid getting sand in their eyes. It blows tentacles of hair across the faces of the beautiful girls, causing them to shriek and blink and teeter on their seven inch heels.

Now, Franco is feeding pizza flour, yeast and water into the dough machine. The wood is burning fiercely in the oven, kicking out extra heat. Despite the fan panting from the top of the fridge, the kitchen is hotter than the sun outside. Franco has a bottle of cold grappa hidden behind the flour bin, where, hopefully, Stefania can't find it. She doesn't understand what it's like to work in the kitchen in this heat. It wrings the moisture out of you quicker than a farmer's wife twisting a wet towel.

Stefania is setting the tables for the first shift, the northern Europeans who like to eat early, bringing their terrible, tired children. Their whingeing and crying aches right through Franco's chest, making a pain in his heart.

Stefania is very good to them, patting their heads, offering candy, ice cream, bending down, using her cajoling voice. Franco realises that it's a long time since she's used that voice with him.

He goes to the door for a moment's respite from the heat and watches the tourists wandering across the piazza with their cameras at the ready; the Germans slung about with expensive kit, the Scandanavians shrouded against the sun, the British with their sad-arses and their little point-and-click Cyber-shots. They are the most recognisable of all. It's the hats that give them away. Babacar's hats you can see immediately, and then the brightly coloured sun hats sold by the souvenir shops. The older men wear straw hats with coloured bands, and the women pale, wide-brimmed wedding hats. The younger men wear baseball caps with Italian inscriptions and fake designer logos they can't translate. Presumably they seem cool to the purchasers, but no Italian would be seen dead wearing them.

Franco fantasises about slogans you could print on the brim that might fool the *stranieri* and raise a snigger in the piazza. *I Fratelli Coglioni*? The balls brothers might sound like a pop band to foreign ears. And what about a red heart and the word *'Finocchio'*? It would show up in their dictionaries as 'Fennel', but what *straniero* would know it was the slang for a gay? He fantasises about a line in the discreet designer labels they are so fond of, perhaps shirts with *Il Piritone* – the big fart – in beautiful script across the pocket. Franco laughs out loud. *Signor Mattachione*, the big joker, that's what they call him sometimes.

As he goes back into the bar, he salutes the Queen of England hanging above the coffee machine. It's a portrait he'd been given by a friend at the British Consulate in Florence when they updated her official image. Her face is serene, her hands folded over her lace dress in an attitude of calm. She stands for the England that Franco remembers when he worked in London as a young *barista* – a country he likes to think is moral and unchanging.

Stefania is in a 'mood'. Last night she had been shouting at him about the state of the house. It's true the kitchen is only half-built and the washing machine is outside under a plastic sheet and you go to bed with building dust on your feet. But it's summer and there's no time between the lunchtime pizzas and the busy evening shift. When you don't get home until 3 o'clock in the morning, you can't get up early to do building work before going down to the pizzeria to start all over again. Franco is exhausted. It's all too much.

'You will have a kitchen by Christmas,' he had promised, as she wept and picked up the bath towel she had just dropped in the dust, that would now have to join the mountain of linen outside waiting to be washed.

'You said that last year,' she had shouted back. 'You promise and promise and don't do anything! It's all fucking words!'

That had shocked him. Stefania doesn't swear like that. She is a girl from the village, gentle, from a good family.

When they were first together, eight years ago,

Stefania's mother had come to the bar where he was working and talked to him very frankly.

'You have a reputation,' she had said. 'You are forty-one. My daughter is only nineteen. I need to know that you are going to treat her well.'

So he had promised and they were married by the priest and Stefania's mother had given them the money for the lease on the pizzeria. In the first two years they had earned enough to buy the little ruined house in Montecolegno from some *straniero* who had romantic ideas about living in Tuscany, but had taken fright at Italian building regulations. Stupid man! How did he not know that you just ignore them and pay the fine at the end? His loss had been Franco's gain.

Simona is standing beside him. She is doing two jobs now – the morning cleaning and the lunchtime shift in the bar before she collects Paolo from school.

'You know I'll not be in tomorrow morning to do the cleaning?'

'*Perché?*'

'It's my court case. Father Hermes is going with me, so maybe I'll get my money from that bastard Vittorio.'

'*Speriamo!* Let's hope so.'

'Father Hermes thinks I should take Paolo with me. Maybe his little face will touch the judge's heart?'

'Maybe.' Franco thinks that judges have hearts of marble.

'And Stefania has written me a very good character.'

Stefania has a fondness for Paolo – she's always feeding him ice cream and cakes and pizza slices when he comes with his mother.

'Will you thank her for me? I can't find her.'

Franco nods. 'She was setting the tables. Maybe she has gone to the supermarket?'

While the dough is proving in the machine he checks to see that Stefania is still nowhere in sight, pours another slug of grappa and sits down on the back step to have a quick joint to get him through the early evening rush.

Biba, the *barista*, comes into the kitchen, her gelled hair sticking up in spikes, her new nose-piercing still an angry red. 'Where's Stefania?'

Franco hastily pinches the ash from the end of the roll-up and puts the stub in his pocket. 'I don't know. There's a problem?'

'The place is filling up and I can't serve the drinks and take orders at the same time. Someone's already complained.'

Franco stands up. 'I haven't seen her since five o'clock.' He comes in and begins to scrape the ash back from the floor of the oven to leave it clean and hot for the first pizzas. He looks towards the hook near the back door, but the car keys are missing. 'Have you tried her phone?'

Biba nods. She's standing on one foot as if paused in mid-flight. 'Her mobile's switched off.'

A voice is calling from the bar. Biba turns. 'I have to go. You'll have to do something – I can't cope on my own!' She vanishes back into the bar.

'*Mamma mia*! Jesus Christ! *Porca dio*! *Vaffanculo* Stefania!' Franco utters every curse he knows. He can feel his bowels loosening, the familiar spasm in his guts. Has she left? Gone? That's something she's never done before.

Biba's head appears round the door frame. She looks desperate. 'You must do something Franco! Four people have just walked out.'

His mobile is in the pocket of his overall. He dials Simona's number. 'Where are you?'

'In the Bar di Pietro.'

'Can you work this evening? We have an emergency! Stefania has vanished and Biba can't manage on her own. Please,' he adds.

'If I can get someone to take Paolo home and look after him for me. I will see.' She sounds reluctant.

'Please,' he says again. He has a feeling that everything is unravelling. Panic. The same feeling he has when he wakes suddenly, alone, in the dark.

Five minutes later Simona walks through the door and takes Stefania's apron down from the hook. She picks up the pad and the pen and then she says, as if it's an afterthought, 'Apparently Stefania went into the Bar di Pietro and made a big drama with Enzo. She called him a shit and everyone was very pleased. Even Eva laughed.'

Simona is slow and she doesn't always write things down correctly. Franco can hear Biba shouting at her. It's almost time to put on some music and have a little fun with the customers, but he feels too tired to be Mick Jagger. He looks at the portrait of the Queen on the wall and makes a little bow. Sorry Ma-am, there will be no British anthem tonight either.

He leaves another message on Stefania's phone. He tries not to sound as if he's begging. He should be angry with her. How could she go off like this and leave them all in the shit?

'There's a man asking if he can talk to Stefania,' Simona says. 'I told him she's not here, so he wants to talk to you.'

A thickset man with a shaven head is standing at the kitchen door. Franco notices that his eyes are swivelling everywhere – looking at the oven, the refrigerator, the steel workbench.

'I've heard you want to sell this place,' he says after a moment.

'Who the fuck told you that?'

The man doesn't answer. He goes into the store-room.

'Hey!' Franco calls after him. 'Get the fuck out of there!' But he's too exhausted to do anything.

The man comes out, a pack of cigarettes in one hand, a lighter in the other. He nods to Franco. 'I'll be in touch,' he says.

'What was that about?' Simona clatters in with a pile of dirty plates.

'Who the fuck knows.' Franco wipes his face on a dish towel. 'There's something very strange going on tonight.'

Simona's holding her hand out. 'Can I have my wages out of the till? I have to go home to Paolo. I promised to be back by twelve.'

Franco waves towards the cash register. 'Help yourself.'

Her eyes widen. Then she sits down at the table opposite. 'Don't you care what happens here?'

Simona's face is swimming in and out of the haze as Franco tries to focus. 'This was my dream, you know. My own place, with Stefania. But now . . .' He makes a gesture. 'She isn't happy and I don't know what to do.'

'Ask her,' Simona says. 'She knows what she wants.'

One of the Swiss tourists is still sitting in a corner of the restaurant with Canadian Rosa and Pierluigi, the *artigiano*. The Albanian boys are outside drinking Fanta. The wind has died down. Franco puts some Bob Dylan on the CD player. When he stands up, Stefania is coming through the door with a strange expression on her face. Franco looks at her and knows that something has changed. Her hair is tangled and she looks as if she's been crying.

'Where have you been?' he yells, though he had meant to say it softly.

'To the hospital with Pia. It was too early, but the baby started to come. She was all alone and frightened so I took her down in the car and then I went to get Matteo. I stayed with her until the baby came.' There are tears running down Stefania's cheeks and dripping down onto her blouse. 'It's a little girl. They are calling her Elena Christiana for her grandmothers.' She throws her bag under the bar and goes into the kitchen. '*Mamma mia*! It's *un casino* in here!'

'Don't leave me,' Franco says, grasping the door frame. 'Please don't. I'll change. I'll do anything you like. But please don't leave me!'

Stefania is stacking the dish-washer. She looks up just for a moment. 'Maybe it's too late for that,' she says in a flat voice, and then she turns her back to put another plate in the rack.

8

Ferragosto

'One night in August, one of those nights disturbed by a
warm and stormy wind . . .'

Cesare Pavese, Feria d'agosto, 1946

The waitress is standing at Carl's elbow with a pad, making
Carl feel rushed. He turns to his wife. 'What would you
like to drink, darling?'

Frida looks at him. 'What are *you* having?'

'Does it matter?' A tinge of irritation creeps into
Carl's voice.

'Nooooh. I just thought . . .'

The girl is becoming restless.

'I'll have a beer. Medium,' Carl says. 'Frida?'

'I was thinking . . . perhaps a prosecco?'

Carl feels a shiver of relief, unaware, until that
moment, of the tension that's been building up inside
him. It's ridiculous to feel like this over ordering a drink.
He'd been afraid – though he knows that's illogical – that
she would order what he ordered, furious that she had
looked, not at the waitress, but at him, as though asking
his permission.

And it's not just the drinks. Carl's become irritated

by the fact that, when Frida dresses, she always seems to choose the same colour that he does. If he's wearing blue, then she will choose something blue; if he wears jeans, she wears jeans; if he wears his black evening trousers and a white shirt, she puts on her little black dress and the white silk shawl she'd bought in India – and they go out like two magpies. This morning he'd put on white trousers and a yellow Ralph Lauren shirt and she'd appeared in white cut-offs and the yellow polka dot affair he'd bought her in that boutique on the Bahnhofstrasse.

There was a similar lack of initiative when they went out sight-seeing. If he wanted to go to a museum she would say, 'Oh, yes, that's a good idea!' or the beach – 'The beach! That's just what I was going to suggest'. It annoys the hell out of him. Does she never have any ideas of her own? He looks at her profile, gazing out across the piazza and wonders what goes on inside her beautiful, well-groomed head. She is as self-contained and closed to him as on the first day they met, twenty years ago, at an advertising symposium in Geneva. A little film she'd made had been on show – good stuff – and there'd been some competition to acquire her, which, of course, Carl had won. She'd been his employee and then his wife and the mother of his child. But since then the life seems to have gone out of her.

Frida is wondering where Michelangelo had sat when he was here. There's a plaque on the wall above her head which the owner of the bar had translated as; *'Michelangelo stayed here when he was working on David'*. She imagines the view would have been much the same. The marble steps of the Duomo, the Lion (she assumes it's a lion) of Florence on a column beside the fountain, the medieval baptistry tucked into the corner of the piazza. It gives Frida a shiver of pleasure to feel part of such continuity – past and present perfectly merged into this one moment – a moment that has already dissolved even as she thinks of it. It makes her feel giddy, or perhaps that's the wine, or the heat.

A group of beautiful girls are walking across the marble paving, like a herd of delicate, exotic animals. One of them is wearing a white dress with a low neckline and a full, short skirt. She's balancing on very high-heeled jade green shoes and holding a matching clutch bag. Frida watches her husband's eyes tracking the girl across the piazza with a twinge of envy. It takes courage to wear a dress like that.

The piazza is full of people – but it's oddly peaceful. Frida can feel the tension of the past few days evaporating from her muscles. There's a juggler performing in the middle of the empty space. He has a whip and he's splitting newspapers held up by a young girl he's just picked out of the crowd, who can hardly hold the paper still for giggling. Just opposite the bar, a man in Tibetan costume is sitting on the steps of the Bank of Rapallo with a large, rather mangy Alsatian dog beside him and a rabbit in a plastic cage. There's a pot in front of him and a notice in three languages that says, 'Save my Dog'.

One of the African street traders is coming towards them. He has a pyramid of coloured hats on his head, belts and bags over his shoulder and an armful of ethnic jewellery. He has a beaming smile on his face as if they are old friends he has only just re-met. 'Hello!' he says, stopping beside their table. 'How're you doin?'

Carl is ignoring him.

Frida finds herself smiling back. 'Where do you

come from?' she asks.

'Senegal. And you? You are English?'

'No. Swiss.'

'Ah ha! You speak my language.' He lapses into a lilting, colonial French.

'Oui.' Frida responds, although she's a German speaker. She doesn't want to disappoint him.

Carl is throwing her an angry glance.

But Frida is looking at the beads the man is carrying. There are necklaces and bracelets made from polished seeds and carved pieces of wood – all in the rich colours of the organic materials that echo the reddish brown of her own hair.

The trader has seen the direction of her gaze. He hands her one of the necklaces. 'Madame, I give you nice price.'

She rolls the knobbly shapes between her fingers. There's something comforting about the feel of the beads in her hand.

'You like that one Madame? For you, ten euro.'

If he's asking ten, she could probably get it for five, but there's no way that Carl would let her wear something that falls into the category of what he calls 'cheap trash'. Reluctantly, Frida shakes her head. 'Sorry, not today.'

The trader doesn't hassle and she likes him for that. 'Another time, Madame. I will be here tomorrow. My name is Babacar. Have a good holiday!'

'For God's sake!' Carl says, as the man moves away, 'Why do you have to encourage these people?'

'I like talking to them. I'd love to know how he got here – how he makes a living. It must be a hard life.'

'I imagine he's an illegal immigrant – it's Europe's biggest problem. You can't even sit outside a bar without being hassled. Give them money and you're just encouraging them.'

Frida braces herself.

Carl says, 'Don't you know that Italy gets more than a hundred boat people a day from Africa? It's ruining the economy.'

Frida says nothing. Things must be pretty bad in Africa, she thinks, if people are prepared to risk their lives to get here, living rough (she imagines he does) and selling cheap trinkets to tourists.

Above the chatter and the bustle of the bar, Frida can hear music. A man is sitting on the steps of the Duomo playing a violin. Schubert – both sad and beautiful at the same time.

She leans across and touches Carl's arm. 'Listen,' she says. 'Isn't that wonderful?'

Carl grunts. 'He's out of tune – look at his hands shaking! Probably a wino.'

But his comments fail to dim Frida's pleasure in the music. She closes her eyes and puts her head back to listen. The music flows into her veins like a transfusion of light. How can something so melancholy feel so uplifting?

Frida can hear the bells of the piazza clock chiming midnight. She lies naked in one half of the gigantic matrimonial bed, burning with a heat that is only partly to do with the temperature of the room. It's too hot even for a sheet. Carl is snoring on the other side of the bed – crashed out after the two bottles of wine over dinner at the Enoteca and then a couple of vintage grappas as a *digestivo*. He's drinking too much at the moment, has put on weight and become puffy round the face. Frida had thought last night that he looked unhappy.

Very quietly, Frida gets up and stands in front of one of the fans. Carl hates air-conditioning. There had been a big argument when they checked into the hotel and he'd demanded these electric fans instead. Apparently it was difficult to close off individual rooms from the 'climatizzazione' that kept the whole hotel at a bearable temperature during what they called the 'Big Heat'. It was Ulysses, the receptionist had explained – a big weather system that blew Saharan dust and equatorial temperatures up from North Africa in August.

Every cell of Frida's body feels as though it's on fire. Her breasts ache. How long is it since Carl touched her? She remembers his fingers rippling down her spine, the silk-soft caress of his hand across her breasts and that deeper caress pushing her further and further into ecstasy. There's an ache in the soft space between her thighs that spreads upwards into her stomach and makes her want to run into the street and offer herself to the first man that passes.

Why has he stopped wanting her? Is he having an affair? Is she no longer attractive?

Frida looks at him, sprawled across the bed, a mesh of grey hairs curled on his chest, the sweat glistening on his skin, his mouth open, his penis draped against his leg, and she thinks that he has the body of an old man. At fifty seven he's already old, whereas she, at forty four, feels hardly used at all.

The fans make a lot of noise. Frida slips on her bra and pants, the linen dress she had worn earlier, and picks up her sandals and purse. The door handle turns in expensive silence and then closes softly behind her.

The piazza is still full of people and the shops

120

appear to be open. Frida wanders around looking in the windows. There's a little dress shop opposite the Duomo with the most beautiful scarves and bags. In one corner of the display is a dress in deep yellow ochre – silk crepe draped across the bodice and around the waist, falling to a flattering mid-calf length. It's condensed sunlight, the colour of Italian stucco. If you wore it with a blue jacket, or a chestnut-brown silk wrap. . . and the African beads – if you bought several strands, they would fill the simple neckline like the beaded collar of an Egyptian princess.

But Carl doesn't like what he calls the 'ethnic look'. He prefers her to wear classic clothes – Hermes, Armani, Max Mara. Frida has learned not to challenge him. She has to look good to impress clients, not to express her own personality. Clothes are important statements of Carl's status.

The pizzeria on the corner is still open. Frida thinks she'll have a cold drink and an ice cream. As she stands in the entrance, hesitating, a man in the white coat and white hat of a pizza chef comes towards her holding out his hands.

'*Ciao bella*! Come in! Come in!'

Before she knows it, Frida is sitting at the bar with a cold prosecco and a tall glass filled with freshly sliced peaches, strawberries and two different colours of ice-cream.

The pizza chef has taken off his hat. 'Why you are on your own?' he asks in stilted English.

'My husband's asleep. He was tired.'

'How can a man be tired when he has so beautiful a wife!' He takes her hand and makes an elaborate pantomime of kissing it. Frida laughs and then notices a woman in an apron standing beside the kitchen door frowning.

121

His name is Franco. He introduces the woman as Stefania, his wife. Her face is set in an expression of discontent.

'You like the English rock music?' Franco asks.

Frida nods. The ice cream is making a cold trail down the inside of her throat.

'Who likes Rolling Stones?' Franco yells across the restaurant.

This seems to be what people have been waiting for. There are cries of 'We do!' Someone begins a chant of 'Mick Jagger! Mick Jagger!' Others join in and some of them are banging their cutlery on the tables.

'Okay. Okay.' Franco slips off his white coat. 'Mick Jagger is in the house.'

He ducks down below the counter of the bar. He seems to be putting a CD in the music machine. When he stands up he's wearing a curly blond wig and holding an empty beer bottle like a microphone.

'Mick Jagger . . .' he breathes into it, and the first thumping beats of *Brown Sugar* begin to pulse out of the speakers.

Franco has a good voice and he can certainly mimic Jagger's writhing pelvic contortions. Frida finds herself laughing and clapping with the rest of them. The noise can probably be heard on the other side of town. A crowd has begun to gather outside, peering in through the windows.

After *Brown Sugar*, Franco does *Satisfaction* and everyone joins in. People are dancing in the piazza. Franco is sweating and his eyes glitter. He's either drunk or he's on something, Frida decides. It's after 2 o'clock when Frida turns the key in the door of the hotel room.

Carl wakes as she slides into bed. 'What're you

doing?' he asks drowsily.

'Too hot to sleep,' she says, but he has already turned over and is slipping back into unconsciousness.

It's like playing truant at boarding school, Frida thinks, sneaking out while the nun's are asleep. How many years ago was that?

Carl has just realised that it's Ferragosto. The day the Italians celebrate the Assumption of the Virgin Mary, or some such shit. It's a bugger, Carl thinks, because everything is closed. Frida likes to go to the beach, so, as there are no alternatives, that's where they are now, in Bagno Seven, an exclusive beach club at Forte dei Marmi. Frida has laid herself out under a gigantic awning with her book and Carl walks restlessly on the edge of the sea. He's tried swimming, but the water is warm and sticky. He could go deeper, but there's a warning on the board about a bloom of jelly fish just off-shore. Even as he thinks about it, he stumbles and just avoids standing on a pink blob, as big as a dinner plate, deflating on the sand.

There are rows and rows of half-naked Italian women under the umbrellas, with pairs of firm brown breasts and pert nipples. The advantage of sun glasses is that no one can tell where, exactly, you're looking. The tiny triangles of fabric draped across their pelvises disguise nothing. Carl can see the proud curve of pubic bone, imagine the neat Brazilian, the moist cleft opening in invitation.

Time for another token dip in the salty soup the Mediterranean has become. Some boys are playing beach ball, throwing their young, taut bodies up to punch the ball across the net. Watching them twists a knot in Carl's

123

gut that requires a medicinal Campari back at the bar. The barman shakes it with fresh orange juice and crushed ice, with just a drop of red Curacao. Carl swallows it, orders another two and takes them out to the beach where Frida lies in the shade. She's asleep with the book on her chest. He puts the glass down beside her, picks up his mobile phone and walks back to the bar.

It's almost empty, except for a middle-aged woman sitting on one of the stools clutching a beer and talking to the barman. At first glance she's not attractive, but his eyes keep being drawn to her.

She's the kind of woman whose skin is tanned to the texture and colour of shoe leather, and she has biceps, for God's sake! And a short, lesbian-style hair cut. Carl can spot them a mile off. He is disconcerted when she turns to include him in her conversation, making an inference about his nationality from his accent. When she talks she has a pretty, rather husky voice and her French is elegant. Once she has established that he's Swiss, she carries on speaking in a careful, but adequate German.

Her name is Shira, she comes from Israel and she runs a marble studio, she tells him – which explains the muscles. It is the best, most exclusive marble studio in the area. They can supply sculptures for cruise ships and office buildings, hotels and public places. Perhaps he has clients who would like a sculpture for their business? It would not only be decorative, but also an investment. Her manner is bold and persistent, but Carl suspects she is very shrewd.

'What about the sculptors,' Carl asks. 'Do you have anyone of note?'

She reels off half a dozen names he recognises. Big names!

Carl orders another Campari cocktail and a beer

for Shira. This could be a good connection. He can see that she is sizing him up, pricing the Piaget Altiplano on his wrist, the Lagerfeld swimwear.

'Come to dinner,' she says eventually.

'Unfortunately tomorrow's our last day.'

'Come tonight. It's Ferragosto so all the restaurants will be fully booked. Unless you have already made arrangements?'

Carl realises that, for the first time in his life, he has not.

When Frida gets back to the hotel's complimentary wi-fi there's an email from Graciella. A big smiley face on her smart phone. 'I hope Dad's behaving himself,' Graciella says. 'How do you like the book? All good here – going to the lake today with Franz and his sister.'

When she thinks of her daughter, Frida feels as though someone has pressed a light switch inside her chest. Graciella is the one really joyful thing in her life. But she's a woman now, pursuing her own life. Graciella has chosen to read American Literature at the University of Basel and she's begun to look outside Europe for her future. There's a boyfriend – a young architect – but Graciella is too pragmatic to tie herself down before she's even learned to fly. Or so Frida hopes.

Before Frida left, Graciella had given her a book of poetry to read on holiday by someone called Adrienne Rich. It's very American, written before Frida was born, and feminist polemic of the kind that Frida had never thought that either her daughter or herself would need to read. But every now and then there's something she recognises. The progress of a love affair. At first, '*No dust upon the furniture of love*', and then the unpaid milkman coming up the stairs. Disillusion. Some time or other the tradesmen always want paying. And then there is a poem about a woman who holds her hand under the hot tap to convince herself that she still exists. There's a round, smooth scar the size of a twenty *centesimo* piece on the palm of Frida's hand where she once held it over a candle to see whether she could still feel anything at all. When Frida looks at Graciella, she recognises her own young self – the enthusiasm, the curiosity, the reaching out across boundaries. Where did it all go?

The water in the shower is beginning to run cold. It's time to get out and dress for the evening.

Carl is on the phone when she comes out of the shower, but he cuts the conversation short. 'The office,' he explains as he puts the phone in his trouser pocket.

'Jana?'

'She's my assistant.' There's a faint exasperated edge to Carl's tone.

I was his assistant once, Frida thinks. There's a hollow feeling under her rib-cage.

'Where are we eating?' Frida asks, opening the wardrobe to inspect the row of neat garments in their plastic covers.

'We're going to someone's house for dinner.' Carl is fastening his cuffs. However hot it is, he won't go out in the evening in short sleeves.

'Oh?'

'I met an Israeli woman in the bar at the beach. She runs a marble studio here and wants to advertise it in Switzerland and Germany. Masterclasses, supported projects – that kind of thing. I said we'd take a look.'

Frida's hand hovers over a plain cream silk shift.

'You promised no business. Remember? This is supposed to be a holiday – just the two of us. No work. You promised!'

'Oh, for God's sake,' Carl says. 'It's hardly business. And I thought you enjoyed meeting interesting people. Anyway, all the restaurants are booked for *Ferragosto*. It's either that or eating in the hotel.'

Frida takes the dress off its hanger. 'I wouldn't have thought a project like that was big enough to interest you.'

Carl grunts. He's examining his chin in the mirror. 'I thought maybe one of the juniors could cut their teeth on it. You can't afford to turn your back on anything in this financial climate. And you never know where it might end.' He turns to pick up his white linen evening jacket. 'Shira's a very interesting woman – top of the class in a man's world apparently. She does household name stuff. So who wouldn't want to work there? All those wealthy ex-wives, bankers retired on full pensions with a sudden urge for creativity. Europe's full of them.'

Shira's house is in the narrow back streets of the town; a double door in a wall that opens into a small courtyard garden crowded with plants in terracotta pots. Frida can hear water hissing and smell the earthy steam coming from the plants as they breathe out the day's heat. Bougainvillea is thrusting its flaming arms towards them, that vulgar shade of purple-pink that no one should ever wear, and the air is sickly with the scent of jasmine.

A table has been set outside. Candles in big glass jars – wine glasses without stems that rock gently on their heavy curved bottoms.

Shira is short and dark, probably in her forties or even fifties, Frida thinks. Quite fierce, with a strong, rough handshake. 'Shall we speak French?' she says straight away. 'We are four nationalities, so perhaps that is best? My English is not very good.'

She introduces a tall, fleshy girl with short, almost masculine hair standing next to her. 'This is Rose Umber. She's from Canada, sculpting here at the moment.'

And then, out of the shadows, a man with dark skin and abundant curly hair steps into the candle light and puts two bottles of wine on the table. Frida estimates that he might be ten years younger than herself – late thirties perhaps.

'Pierluigi,' Shira says, waving him towards Carl and Frida. 'My best *artigiano*. There's nothing he can't reproduce in marble.'

He holds Frida's hand for just a second longer than is necessary – his eyes flick up and down as if they like what they see. Then he grasps Carl's hand.

Frida knows that Carl has been worrying about the quality of the food he's likely to get in someone's house. He had stopped at the Enoteca and bought a couple of bottles of wine to ensure that at least he has something decent to drink. He insists that Shira open it first and Frida wonders if she's offended. But the food is delicious. Local prosciuto, sliced so thin you can see through it, lardo, salty and sharp on coarse Italian bread, and there are fresh anchovies marinated in oil, garlic and lemon juice. Frida sucks her fingers and smiles at Pierluigi over the table.

Carl is talking figures and percentages, discussing the intricacies of putting a value on reputation in the art world and grilling Pierluigi on his training. 'People need to know they're with someone they can trust.' He sounds uncomfortable talking in French, as if his mouth can't form the fluid, musical vowels properly.

Pierluigi is telling him about the years he has spent learning how to carve marble – the apprentice pieces he had to do, carving lace cushions and folds of fabric and the heads of children. Now he's learning how to operate digital laser cutters and 3-D printers.

Then, just as a plate of pasta with salmon and asparagus is put in front of them, Shira suddenly turns her attention away from Carl.

'So what do you do?' she asks Frida, as if she really wants to know.

Unprepared, Frida hesitates for a moment and feels the conversation pause around her. She puts down her fork. 'Originally, I studied graphic design and worked in advertising. I was Carl's assistant.'

'And now?'

'I left to have a child and didn't go back.'

'Why? Didn't you enjoy it?'

'Oh, I loved it. But . . .' She glances at Carl, who is frowning down at his plate. 'I stayed at home for my daughter. I don't regret it . . .' Frida finds herself unable to go on without stumbling. Is that true? Is what she's feeling regret? She recovers herself quickly. 'I stayed, but now that she's left home to begin her own life, I think I'd like to do something again.' Frida's fork rattles against her plate. She is trembling with the effort of making such an admission.

Shira gives her a measuring look over her glass of wine. 'So, how would you see the advertising? What would appeal to women like yourself? Women with time and money?'

'Bored with their lives,' Frida adds recklessly.

129

The wine is making her bold, or perhaps it's the French language. Carl won't like it. There's a certain rigidity in the way he's sitting that doesn't bode well. Frida allows Pierluigi to top up her glass. 'Glossy magazines, I suppose. The kind that are all about creating beautiful homes and the weekend ones with adverts for art exhibitions and painting classes. Then there's the internet – Facebook – websites – women with time on their hands spend a lot of it surfing the net on their iPads.' She takes a deep breath. 'But the best advertising is to get someone to make a short documentary film about the studio. Something romantic that shows the kind of history you have here.'

Frida wonders what happened to the friends she had begun to work with after university – Zara and Matt and Simon. Bellavista they had called themselves. She knows the company still exists, but she lost touch with the people long ago as their lives diverged.

Carl has noticed that Pierluigi's eyes keep flicking back to Frida. Once it had been a source of pleasure, watching other men desire what he possessed, but now . . . It isn't like Carl to feel insecure – it makes him feel queasy.

Another glass of wine and he realises that the queasy sensation in his stomach is more than just a disturbance of mood. Shira has a halo round her head and Carl's aware that he is having to concentrate very hard on what she's saying. Too late to regret the anchovies, which had tasted quite strong to his sensitive palate.

There's a fine pecorino cheese on the table, crumbly with a thick grey crust, and some ripe pears and little almond pastries. But Carl suddenly feels unable to eat anything.

The stone walls are reflecting back the searing heat they absorbed during the day and there's no breeze in the courtyard at all. Sweat is trickling down Carl's back and the feeling is very unpleasant. No one else seems to be conscious of the heat. Frida looks particularly cool in her creamy silk dress with the gold straps that sit so neatly over her delicate collar bones. Thank God she's stayed thin! Carl looks at Canadian Rose whose ample breasts are mutineering in a sack-like shift of blue cotton. She's amicably telling him about a commission she has just been given for a marble piece in Ottowa, how much she's learned here from the skilled artisans.

'Such a tradition,' she's saying. 'Their great, great, many great-grandfathers worked for Michaelangelo!'

Jana would enjoy doing something like this, Carl thinks. There's no money in it, but the art world is a new area to get into. Shira is dropping some big names – if any one of them needed P.R. . . .

Carl asks for a glass of iced water which Shira brings from the kitchen with a slice of lemon suspended among the crushed fragments. He notices that his hand is shaking a little as he takes it from her. Has he drunk so much? The cocktails this afternoon at the beach, the aperitivos in the bar earlier, the numerous top-ups of red wine. Nothing he isn't used to. But then there's the heat, and the anchovies . . . Carl's vision is unaccountably foggy and there's an ominous lurch in his stomach. He needs to stand under a cold shower and then lie horizontal, absolutely still, in a quiet place. It's embarrassing to say the least. To leave the dinner so early, so abruptly, might even be construed as rude.

'Are you all right?' Frida asks, in German, leaning across the table. 'You look very pale.'

131

'Not too good. Feeling the heat a bit.'

'You were out too long in the sun this afternoon.'

Carl realises that, whether polite or not, it's necessary to leave. The effort of speech makes him so nauseous he has to close his mouth. It's difficult to stand up.

'I'm very sorry,' he can hear Frida say, 'but my husband is feeling unwell. I think we'd better go back to the hotel. We aren't used to this heat – it was more than forty degrees this afternoon.'

Everyone is suddenly solicitous.

'You must stay,' Carl hears himself say to Frida. 'It's only five minutes walk. I'll be fine.'

'Perhaps the walk will do you good?' the Canadian girl says. 'I'll go with you and your wife can stay and talk. I'm living in an apartment right next to the hotel. It's no trouble.'

Out in the street there's a faint movement of air, only just discernible. It's not so difficult to breathe out here. Except that the walls are swaying and every now and then the paved street threatens to come up towards him. The girl has a warm hand on his elbow. She's chatting about her work. He must come and see it at the studio tomorrow. Her voice goes through his head like wire.

The hotel doorway, the ice cool lobby, have never been more inviting. Carl says something to his escort, he doesn't know what, and stumbles towards the lift. It was the anchovies, he thinks. A bad anchovy.

Frida feels guilty. She should have gone with him – supposing he isn't just drunk but really ill? Supposing he has a stroke, or a heart attack? How would she feel if she went back later and he was lying on the bathroom floor? How could she live with herself? But I'd be free, a tiny rebellious voice says at the back of her brain. And a sensation, just a little like happiness, shoots through her mind for a second, until she knocks it down. She is horrified by her own self-ishness. Anyway, he has only drunk too much – the combination of alcohol and heat – dehydration – tomorrow he will have the hangover from hell.

'Tomorrow morning,' Shira is saying. 'Would you like to see the studio? You can talk to some of the people about their work – see the kind of experience we offer.'

'I would love to,' Frida says – acutely aware that she has just used the 'I' word. Would Carl want to? Does it matter? She wants to. *Je veux.* I want, I want, I want. French is such a seductive language. Everything seems possible.

Shira is talking to her as if she's a partner in Carl's business, as if she matters. As if she's going to be the one handling this project. If only.

After the coffee, Frida gets up to go regretfully. Shira kisses her on both cheeks. 'See you tomorrow,' she says. 'About ten?'

'I'll walk you back,' Pierluigi says.

It's almost midnight but the streets are thronged with people.

'Doesn't anyone sleep here?' Frida asks.

He laughs. 'This is when people come out to play. It's too hot during the day.'

'And the shops are still open!'

'They want to catch the after-dinner trade – it's a short season here, there's not much going on in the winter. People struggle.'

As they near the hotel he asks, 'A night cap in the piazza?'

Frida hesitates and then says, 'Yes, why not. But I'd better check up on Carl first.'

The room is dark and the fans sound like a million birds' wings threshing the air. There's the acid smell of vomit. Carl is lying face down on the edge of the bed, one arm dangling, breathing noisily.

'He's asleep,' Frida says, rejoining Pierluigi in the street. 'I'm afraid I'm still wide-awake. I've not been sleeping well lately.'

'Problems?'

'One or two.' Does she look so obviously unhappy that even a stranger at a dinner party can pick it up.

'So why aren't you happy?' Pierluigi asks as they sit outside the bar.

Frida turns her glass round and round on the table. She's recklessly drinking some kind of fruit cocktail she'd seen the waiter delivering to someone else.

'I don't really know,' she says at last. 'It's as though I'm living someone else's life, inside someone else's skin and I don't like that person at all.'

'What are you going to do about it?'

'I don't know that either. Break out maybe, do something crazy . . . I imagine doing that sometimes. But every day goes by and I don't do anything – it's as though I'm waiting for something to happen. What about you?'

'Oh, I'm very happy. I'm doing just what I want to do. My parents wanted me to be a doctor, but I've always wanted to carve marble. I think they'd have accepted it if I'd been a sculptor, but an *artigiano* – someone who works with his hands . . . they still don't like it.'

'Could you not have been a sculptor?'

'I tried, but I'm not an ideas man. Much happier dealing with someone else's.'

'Married?' Dear god, what is she thinking of?

'No!' He laughs. 'A few near misses. I like to be independent. There are too many interesting opportunities.'

Pierluigi is looking at her in a way that makes Frida's skin prickle with goosebumps. 'You have beautiful hair,' he says suddenly.

'Thank you.' She stands up. 'I must go.'

'Have I frightened you away?'

'No.' She smiles down at him. 'There's something I want to buy in a boutique over there and I want to catch them before they close. Thank you for the drink.'

'My pleasure.'

'And I will see you tomorrow?'

'Certainly. I'll be at the studio.'

Carl opens his eyes. It's daylight. He can see that Frida is standing at the bottom of the bed.

'Do you feel up to having some breakfast?' She looks anxious.

Carl attempts to lift his head from the pillow and quickly shuts his eyes again. 'Is there any water in the mini bar?'

He can hear the fridge door open and shut and then a small bottle of San Pellegrino appears on the bedside cabinet.

'It's our last day . . .' Frida says.

Carl doesn't know what he's supposed to answer.

'I said we'd be at the studio at ten.'

'Then you'll just have to cancel. That's the last time I have bloody anchovies.'

He can hear Frida move towards the door.

'I'll come back after breakfast,' she says.

Frida thinks that Rose seems disappointed that Carl isn't with her when she arrives at the studio, but Frida makes a point of admiring her work – not that it's difficult. Rose is carving a piece of marble in a beautiful pelagic quartz in shades of pink and grey – the polished face revealing the fossil traces of prehistoric sea creatures. It's pitted with little holes that give it the quality of lace.

'Can I touch?' Frida asks and Rose nods, smiling as Frida runs her fingers over the curved surfaces.

'What do you call it?' she asks.

'*La serena*. The mermaid.'

'It's very beautiful.'

'Shira says I can put it in the exhibition in December. Then it's going to Ottowa to sit in someone's garden.'

'A nice commission!'

'Isn't it? I was so lucky. It was a man who runs a gallery in Canada and he came here to see someone else's work. Life is so much serendipity – don't you think?'

The studio isn't what Frida had expected. There are large ramshackle sheds with corrugated roofs and walls assembled from sheets of fibre board and aluminium. There's dust everywhere, haphazard piles of stone, unfamiliar machines and air hoses and percussion drills – it's noisy and dirty and chaotic.

Two of the biggest sheds at the end of the yard are locked. 'These are for secret work,' Pierluigi says. 'We do things for some of the best international artists – Bottero, Kano, Miteraj, Hirst. But it has to be secret. No one is allowed in except the *artigiani* working on the project.'

'So why do you need to advertise if you have such

136

big names here?'

'Ah.' He pauses and smiles. Frida can see him phrasing what he says. 'The art world has hit a bad patch – not so many people having commissions done. And the big names are all beating us down on price because they know we need the work. Some of the big guys have gone to cheaper locations – eastern Europe, even Asia. Fewer artists are carving marble or using the foundries here.'

'That's sad. Rose was telling me about the tradition. It would be tragic if it died out.'

'Very. Once there would have been at least two dozen sculptors working here and double that number of *artigiani* helping them – as well as working on their own projects. We used to be commissioned to make copies of statues and fountains and church fonts – now no one orders such things.'

He takes her arm and his touch makes her tremble. 'Come and let me show you something.'

There's a stone building at the back of the yard where Shira has her office. An outside staircase leads up to the top floors. Pierluigi unlocks a sturdy door. Inside there's a kind of twilight – there are windows but they're obscured by dust and by the objects piled in front of them. A statue of Puccini stands beside the door with his hand raised like a ticket collector. Next to him on a wooden box there's a devil and an old woman. Venus, minus her arms, reclines against the wall, three dolphins, a dwarf, several urns, columns and benches, half-clothed women draped in white, babies and leering *putti*, severe looking men in civic robes. Pierluigi points out Garibaldi, Carducci, Vittorio Emanuele, Giordano Bruno, Cosimo Medici. A soldier in a tin hat lies with his rifle, bayonet fixed, staring up at a Madonna. Another soldier stands in full American combat kit next to a rearing horse and a large sea creature that seems to be part of a fountain.

'They're all made in plaster,' Pierluigi says. 'You could come up here and choose whatever altar piece or memorial you wanted. Something for your garden, or your house. And the *artigiani* would carve it for you. But no one wants them any more.'

It's surreal, like a film set for a horror movie, or being inside a very peculiar mind. Beside the flaring nostrils of a giant horse's head, there's a figure of Pan with shaggy legs and an engorged priapus. Frida can't resist running her fingers along its length, before becoming aware of Pierluigi watching her. She blushes.

He's smiling. 'Not everything was commissioned by the church,' he says, and as he speaks he puts a hand gently on her shoulder.

Frida can feel the heat of his fingers against her skin and she shivers.

He takes his hand away. 'Forgive me.'

But she turns towards him, shocked by her own daring. 'No, it's not that. It's just that no-one's touched me in a long time. My husband . . .' Frida remembers that last, fumbling attempt at intercourse in a Spanish hotel and makes a despairing gesture.

'That's a crime,' he says. 'You are a beautiful woman.' He puts out a hand to caress her cheek and when she doesn't move away, slides his hand down to her breast. He pulls her close with the other hand on her buttocks, holding her tight against him, thigh to thigh, so that she can feel the change from soft to hard through the thin fabric of her dress.

'I've wanted to do this ever since I saw you at dinner last night,' he says.

Frida feels her breast begin to harden under his hand. Shaking with desire, she opens her mouth to receive his tongue, the sharp tip caressing the inside of her cheek, playing joyfully with her own.

After a while he lifts his head and looks towards an old sofa against the wall, covered in sheets. 'Do you mind a little marble dust?' he asks.

She begins to orgasm almost the moment he enters her and then he is shuddering inside her, and her whole body goes through spasm after spasm of pleasure that takes control of her entirely. Her legs tremble and she bites into his shoulder to stop herself crying out.

'You have a lot of passion,' he says afterwards, zipping up his trousers. 'You should use it.'

Frida is staring at the cracked ceiling and the cobwebs glimmering with reflected light. 'I'm thinking of staying on here.'

'I hope this isn't anything to do with me!' He sounds shocked.

Frida is tempted to laugh at the expression on his face. 'Haven't you got something going with Rose?'

'You're observant! But it's all in the past. She's very single-minded about her work.' There is hurt in his eyes, quickly shut out.

It's love that messes everything up, Frida thinks. Sex is less complicated.

Pierluigi holds out his hand to pull her up from the couch. 'If you're serious about staying on, I know someone who's renting out a room. Her name's Anastasia. Rose was going to take it until someone lent her an apartment. I could give you her phone number.'

Carl feels better after his sleep, an afternoon at the swimming pool and a long gin and tonic in the bar. But Frida is in an odd mood.

'Did you take any notes for Jana this morning?' he asks.

She taps the side of her head. 'No. It's all in here.'

'You haven't forgotten we've got the Weigler's coming for dinner on Saturday?

Frida's eyes flicker, so perhaps she has.

'And I had a text from Graciella. She'll be there tomorrow with that idiot Franz.'

Frida looks as if she's about to cry. 'Why do you call him that? He's a nice boy.'

'He's an idiot. One of these days she'll wake up and realise it.'

Frida is looking at him in a way that Carl finds unsettling. She seems frightened, abstracted. Is she not well? There was definitely something wrong with the fish last night. It's always a risk eating in someone's house, particularly in this heat.

'Are you all right?' he asks.

The merest twitch of the head.

'Are you ill?'

'Nothing I can get a prescription for.'

The bloody African is beside their table again, grinning at Frida and brandishing his shoddy wares.

'I give you nice price madame.'

Frida is smiling at him. 'Ah, Babacar. Let me see.'

And the next moment she has an armful of bloody trinkets and is handing over thirty euros.

'I don't know where you think you're going to wear

those.'

'Oh, I'll find somewhere.' She's putting her purse away in her bag and her hair falls forward across her face, hiding her expression.

It's probably the heat – the holiday. Carl remembers the last time they went away together – that weekend in Barcelona. She'd behaved very strangely there too. It will be all right again when they get back to Zurich. Carl looks at his watch. 'I've booked a table at the Enoteca,' he says.

Frida's head comes up. 'I hate that place! It's so pretentious.'

'You've never said anything before. What's got into you?'

'Nothing.'

'And what were you doing all morning with that *artigiano*? The guy who was staring at you all evening over dinner. You were away for hours. What was his name?'

'Pierluigi.' She sounds very calm, and then she says, with a distinct edge to her voice, 'Probably just what you do with Jana.'

He stares at her in amazement and just for a moment her eyes hold his completely steady as if she's reading him from the inside out.

Carl stands up suddenly and his chair falls backwards. 'I'm going back to the hotel.' He picks up his wallet. 'I booked the table for eight thirty if you can be bothered to come.'

Frida has a strange, sick feeling under her ribs as she watches Carl walk across the piazza to the hotel. Her legs tremble when she thinks about what she's been fantasising about doing. But how can she even contemplate not being there when Graciella comes home tomorrow for the usual weekend family meal? And then Frida remembers the poems her daughter had given her. Perhaps Graciella will understand.

Franco is at her elbow. 'You want another drink?'

'Please. Do you have anything to make one brave?'

'Ah. What the English call the Dutch Courage.' He laughs. 'I bring you.'

What arrives looks like a Mojito, with a handful of mint among the cracked ice, but darker in colour. It smells very strongly of rum. There are slices of fruit floating on top and slices of pineapple and orange spiked on the rim. She can feel her spine stiffening after the first sip.

'You stay for a pizza?' Franco asks. He's been inviting them since they first came, but pizzas aren't on Carl's list of permissible foodstuffs.

'I'll stay,' Frida says, feeling her heart thud inside her chest. So this is how it is to be alone. She takes Babacar's beads out of her bag and begins to thread them round her neck. They're warm, as if they've been out in the sun.

Pierluigi is coming across the piazza with Rose and a tall blonde girl she doesn't know.

'Can we join you?' Rose asks.

'Please.'

And suddenly Frida is in the middle of a casual, laughing group. She pictures Carl at the Enoteca, alone among the white linen and the silver service, and just for a moment feels sadness. She should get up and go and join him, but it's too late.

It's after midnight when Frida gets back to the hotel and Carl is already snoring, sprawled across the bed with the fans whirring on the maximum setting.

Her cases, packed this afternoon, are neatly stacked beside the dressing table. She has only to take her wash-bag from the bathroom and put it with her dress in the shoulder bag. The beads make a soft, clicking waterfall sound as she slips them in, but Carl's breathing doesn't falter. Her travel clothes are laid out on a chair – black stretch trousers and a loose shift. She has Anastasia's address in her handbag and the name of a good hotel in Florence.

Carl's wallet is lying on the edge of the dressing table. Frida stands and looks at it, holding her breath. Then she puts out a hand and picks it up. There are several credit cards he hardly ever uses – ones he won't miss for a while. She could take money out on each of them, enough to survive for a few weeks, until she can decide what to do. She slides the cards from their leather sheaths. Sometimes there is more than one in each compartment, so the gaps aren't noticeable. She puts the wallet back in exactly the same position. It feels like theft, but she has to tell herself – I have earned this money. I have earned it. With this money I'm going to buy back my soul.

Then she slings the bag over her shoulder, picks up the two suitcases and softly, very softly, opens the door.

9

A Wanderer in Many Lands

When you really listen, David thinks, it's possible to hear music in everything. If you close your ears to the words, the voices in the piazza become a fugue of pitch and percussion – a kind of abstract polyphony. At night it's the sound of feet ringing in the station underpass, an approaching train singing on the metal rails, the wind making an aeolian harp out of the swinging clock.

Now it's the bell in the campanile – a reverberating B – just off the note, almost flat. David holds the note in his head as he lifts the violin onto his shoulder, the bow poised over the strings, waiting for the moment when the bell stops.

The marble steps of the Duomo are warm through his thin trousers, giving back the heat of the afternoon sun. The day has been hot and the air in the piazza is oppressive. David's limbs feel exhausted from the weight of it.

The last echoes of the bell die away. David flexes his fingers and lowers the bow onto the strings.

It's the first pure note that matters, coming straight from the soul, like an arrow, towards the hearts of the people walking past. Most of them don't stop talking, slipping a coin into his violin case as they pass without making eye contact. But occasionally someone will pause for a moment to listen.

The woman in the grey linen dress has closed her eyes at the café table and David can tell that her whole body is turned towards the music. Tonight he will play for her. She looks sad, so perhaps the Schubert – something to help her enter her sadness, because David has learned that when you are unhappy, you have to go into it like a dark cave, and let the darkness wash over your head, until it gives up its secrets. Only then will it let you go.

It's the dreams you have to beware of, because in sleep you can no longer control the mind. At night, lying awake on the marble bench in the waiting room at the abandoned station, David tells himself stories to keep away the false dreams that slink unbidden through the Gates of Ivory.

Once upon a time, he murmurs, once upon a time; a formula of comfort that creates distance and certainty. For there was once a time when he belonged to a tribe – a flock of black and white birds who assembled night after night, year after year, to create music. Sometimes, even when he's awake, he still hears it – that commanding tap, tap. And then the silence. And in that silence comes the fear that dries his throat and paralyses his fingers.

But it was only once upon a time, and he knows now that if you can tell yourself the story of your own life you can change the story at any point in the narrative. And now he is in a new story and a new time.

After he's played for a while and the tourists have drifted away to the restaurants or back to their hotels, David goes into the bar where he knows Matteo will have a drink waiting for him and a plate of left-over snacks which he always offers casually – 'If you don't eat them they will only go in the bin'. David sits in a corner and eats quietly and efficiently.

Outside, Babacar is circling the tables – a pyramid of hats on his head, his shoulders draped in belts and scarves. He carries a circular wheel of cigarette lighters wound together with elastic and drags a shopping trolley behind him loaded with handbags and other goods. His face beams a white smile framed by his chocolate skin. David watches him targeting people – the high-five greeting – 'Hi there, how you doin'?' The casual sales patter made to sound almost a joke. The easy way he accepts rejection – 'Okay. Next time. Next time.' – keeping a smile fixed on his face. There, David thinks, is a life harder than his own. He has seen Babacar sleeping in bus shelters and on the steps of the Misericordia.

Now Babacar has stopped beside the woman in the grey linen dress that David had noticed earlier. The man beside her is saying something forcefully to Babacar and making signs with his hands, but the woman is shaking her head and, as David watches, she puts out an arm and points to something on Babacar's trolley. It's a string of African beads carved in wood. The woman has them in her fingers, but some kind of altercation is going on and Babacar seems uncomfortable, shifting from one foot to the other, adjusting the pyramid of hats on his head.

Then the woman takes some money out of her bag and presses it into Babacar's hand. The man turns his head away. A group of people come out of the Pizzeria at that moment and begin to say noisy goodbyes so David doesn't see what happens next. When they've moved on, only the woman is sitting at the table with her drink. The man has gone.

The Albanian boys are leaving the bar. Nico swaggers out without looking, but Zamir stops at David's

147

table and says, in awkward Italian – 'We are going to the caravans. Come and play. We have also a friend who brings music.'

The word for caravan in Italian is *ruolotte,* which David speculates must have some relationship to *ruote,* the word for wheels. And there they stand, the houses on wheels, a crazy assortment of caravans donated to Brother Hermes by their former owners. Small, large, battered, pristine. There is even an old American trailer, cigar-shaped and silver, dumped here by who-knows-what crazy adventurer. Brother Hermes has European money to rent the land and the blessing of the *comune* because it keeps people from sleeping in the streets – poverty discreetly kept out of sight for the wealthy tourists they depend on for their income.

Brother Hermes had offered David a berth in one of the vans if he'd been willing to share. But he'd refused. Even when he'd been travelling with the orchestra, it had been separate rooms, no sharing, and when he'd been in a relationship, learning to sleep with someone was the most difficult thing. The old station, just outside the town walls, suits him. It's been closed for two years; the waiting room and ticket hall padlocked and empty. There is only a platform and an automatic ticket machine and fewer trains stop there now, but the water is still connected to the washroom and David has managed to work the door loose and fit his own padlock to avoid the mess of discarded needles, plastic bottles, cigarette packets and dead leaves that drift into the derelict rooms. He can sleep there undisturbed.

The *ruolotte* camp set up by Brother Hermes is in one of the disused marble studios. There are skips full of marble fragments and, in the tin-roofed sheds against the fence, old machinery has been abandoned to rust. The caravans have been parked between stacks of marble blocks left behind when the sculptors and artisans departed. The boys have rolled some of the blocks into the centre as improvised benches round an oil drum where they've lit a fire. It seems strange to have a fire in August, but the light it generates flickers on their faces and reflects from the white vans giving enough illumination to play by.

Zamir has his button accordion and another boy, Rumanian perhaps – he has the look of a Roma – is playing a small tin flute. David tunes his violin to its pitch and then tries to follow the wild variations of this Eastern-European gypsy music. It's the music of exile; the aching minor chords, the dissonances, the wailing phrases that seem to bring the entire plain of central Europe, from Hungary to Siberia, into the ears. But it's also music for dancing and Nico and Rezar lead the others in an energetic but stately choreography with much foot stomping and hand clapping. A dance for men only, one that is not about seduction, but about virility and showmanship. David can feel the music in his fingertips and trembling along his bow. Regret for something lost, an affirmation of belief, an echo of hope. Then, suddenly, he's exhausted. Light-headed. It's time to go back to his pitch on the station bench in the deserted waiting room.

David has always been able to see things hidden from other people. As he walks he can see the vapour rising from the marble pavement of the piazza in red and gold plumes like the flaming emissions of some mythical beast. The shops and bars are shimmering in a purple haze – the walls bending and swaying as if to their own music. At first, the movement is comforting and soothing, but underneath there is something else, a jarring, discordant note that ripples through the paving beneath his feet making him rock slightly as he walks.

At the entrance to the underpass, David stops. He thinks he can see two men standing at the entrance, dark shapes, half-hidden in the semi-darkness. The lights in the underpass seem to have been extinguished and the tunnel is filled with grey fog. David knows that the men are waiting for him. For a moment he's paralysed, unable to decide what he should do. His stomach cramps with fear. He turns to run.

Back in the piazza, he can see that a door to the underworld has been opened in the Michelangelo Tower behind Franco's pizzeria. It gapes black in the darkness, but David is drawn towards it in spite of his fear. He thinks he can hear murmuring voices inside. 'Come in, come in,' they say in the Italian language. 'Welcome. . . we have been waiting for you.' It's very cold here, deep under the piazza – the coldness of the catacombs.

The men must be in front of him now because he can see two cigarette ends burning in the darkness. And the pale shadow of a face with dark sockets for eyes. They have come for him. They are going to break his bones all over again. In the darkness he thinks he can hear someone crying.

Then he hears Franco's voice – a little slurred. '*Ciao* David!'

As he moves forward out of the darkness into the pool of light spilled by the candle, Franco is holding out his hand. 'Have a smoke.' He's offering a joint and grinning.

'You've found me out,' Franco says. They are sitting side by side on an old wooden bench. The ceiling drips.

'This is where I keep my stash, and the grappa

Stefania doesn't know about. You want a drink?'

David tries to shake his head but it feels enormous and barely attached to his body. He makes a negative movement with his hand but that, too, seems unsteady.

'It's amazing no one uses this place,' Franco says, leaning back against the damp wall as if in an armchair. 'You can go all the way to La Rocca from here.' He passes the joint to David again and stands up. 'You need to take better care of yourself my friend. You must eat more. Come upstairs and I will make us both a pizza.'

The fire in the oven is almost out, but you can still feel the enormous heat. David holds his hands out in the opening, while Franco throws the dough. He drops the first attempt and it lands over the coffee machine. It looks like a woman in a white dress with her head in her hands. Franco is almost paralysed by laughter as he tries to lift it off. He slugs another shot of grappa.

'She has left me, you know. . . Stefania.' There's a pause.

'Well, not left, exactly . . .' He slops tomato sauce onto the misshapen dough. 'She has told me to get out. At the end of the month, I have to go. She has sold my share of the business to a man from Pisa, so from next month there will be no more Franco pizzas.'

Franco carries on answering the questions David doesn't ask. 'What will I do?' He pushes David aside to slide the long handled board balancing the pizza inside the oven. He's sweating profusely.

'I am going to go to some friends in England. London. That is where you come from. No?'

David makes an indefinite movement with his head. He no longer comes from anywhere. When he is here, he is here. When he is not, he is not.

Franco sits at the plastic table with the grappa in front of him. He holds out a glass. David's mouth feels dry. 'I have to go,' he manages to say and stumbles out through the door.

The flames have died down in the piazza. The pavement still glows, but the buildings have stopped dancing. He turns towards the underpass. They have put the lights back on. It's empty.

There are no trains so late – but someone is on the station platform. When he gets closer he sees it's the woman who was in the bar earlier. She jerks her head round at his footsteps. He can see her aura flickering from grey to blue – the colours of fear and insecurity.

'It's okay,' he says in English. It's an effort to speak because his tongue is so swollen it's blocking his mouth. His lips feel numb as he tries to form the words. 'You know there are no trains until morning?'

'I know.' Her voice, strongly accented, sounds thick, as if she has been crying. 'I came to look at the time-table. I was thinking of Florence, but there isn't a train until six o'clock. And then I thought I'd wait here.'

'Are you afraid?'

She shrugs. 'More afraid of what I've left. If I go back I might not have the courage to get away again.' She pauses and walks restlessly along the platform – a few paces one way and then back. 'You sleep here?' she asks.

David nods. In the dim glow of the street lighting through the window he can see that she's appalled.

'What kind of life is that?' she asks, in a tone of contempt, indicating the back-pack, the violin, the sleeping bag, and he knows she thinks that he has nothing.

'Freedom,' David says, but he doesn't add what he is thinking. He looks at her elegantly cut clothes, her expensive shoes, the straight fall of her long hair and knows that this is someone who never travels with less than 30 kilos of luggage. And even if there is no longer a husband, she will always have someone. She's that kind of woman.

'We're supposed to be leaving in the morning,' she says suddenly. 'But I can't bear to go. Italy is so beautiful. I feel as though I belong – as though I've been waiting all my life for this.'

David hears a sarcastic bark – his own – and then his voice saying. 'This is a town that people come to when they've nowhere else to go. We drift up here like wreckage on a beach. It's a town of migrants and *stranieri*.'

'What do you do in winter?' she asks.

'I go south, to Sicily, to keep warm.'

David goes around the back to use the toilet, carefully undoing the padlock and then locking it again after him. When he comes out, she's gone. He feels a certain relief, but also regret. It's not your problem, he tells himself, other people's relationships. Unhappy souls.

September – the mornings are cool and the lamps are still lit in the street when the café opens. It's becoming too cold to sleep on the marble benches of the station. A cool breeze picks up in the evening and a faint silver aura clings to the oleanders on the other side of the track. David feels very conscious of being caught up in something older than our mechanical calculations of time. The world turns, the sun and the moon oscillate in the sky, the universe – tipsy and infinite – whirls a procession of constellations overhead.

Thousands of years of human existence on the hills above the town have left their impressions on the landscape. People used to live like goats up there on the mountains – high up in the caves at the upper limit of the tree line – where, on humid days, the jagged crags of rock are hidden in white vapour. David thinks of them as the cloud-dwellers – ancient people whose spirits cling to the trees and the rocks and the streams they once venerated. Sometimes he feels very close to them. There are days when he feels more spirit than flesh, as if his own physical manifestation was fading – about to dissolve its atoms back into the elemental components of the planet. Sometimes he imagines, when he looks at his hand holding the bow, that he can see right through it, as if he has no substance.

When he feels like that he knows that it's time to visit the cloud-dwellers. He goes up the path from the town, following the old paved way, the masonry of the wall so tight you can hardly fit a blade of grass between the stones, to a small plateau on the shoulder of the mountain. Here there is a shallow carved basin with a worn face above it in the rock, like a lion's face with a mane of hair, or a wild man of the forest, half animal, half human. Sometimes David thinks he sees a woman's face in the slant of the eyes, a softness around the mouth, where water trickles into the stone bowl. Something about it, something secret and wise, tells him that it's very old, older than the Romans, something that has an affinity with the strange figures left behind by the vanished people of the Luni – distant and magical – connected to the forest and the rock, caught between the earth and the sky.

David likes to sit here, looking out across the plain, across the roofs of the town, out to sea and the

154

Tuscan islands. He can hear the *ghiri* in the trees, the droning of cicadas, the mewing cries of the snake eagles circling overhead, gathering together before their autumn migration. Sometimes he feels so part of it all he thinks the earth might just fold him into itself and he can feel his body settling, taking on the shape of the ground beneath him.

And sometimes he thinks he can hear the roots striking down through the thin soil, splitting the rock apart as they grope their way into the cracks made by the water, forcing its way through subterranean channels. Then he smokes a joint to stop his hands from shaking, takes out the violin and allows his bow to shape the sounds, the notes sliding between the shadows of the two worlds past and present.

David has always wondered how the swallows make up their minds to fly south from the telegraph lines in England. What was it about that particular day out of all the others? Now he knows. It's a feeling in the blood, a restlessness that gathers as the weather cools and the nights lengthen. Then, one day, you wake up and you know it's time to leave.

It hasn't been a good summer. There's no money for the ferry to Palermo, so he must hitch his way south on the lorries. He picks up his back-pack, ties his sleeping bag to the strap, and carries his violin case in his hand. Matteo has given him two brioches and a focaccia to put in his pocket. On the bus to the autostrada service station David looks back at the old walls of the town and the crowned dome of the cathedral. This year, there's a feeling of sadness. For the first time he's leaving somewhere looking back, not forward; as if this is the last time.

10

The Pope's Red Shoes

It's the day the mirror will fall down in the shop. But Olimpia doesn't know that when she wakes as usual at six o'clock, in darkness, without the aid of an alarm. Her sister Marina is still sleeping on the other side of the bed. Olimpia and her sister have slept together for the whole of their lives. They are careful not to touch each other, keeping to their own spaces on opposite sides of the mattress. Since they were children, they have turned their backs to each other, pulled the sheets over their heads and closed their ears to the private sounds of sobbing and moaning, and the other, darker, bodily sounds that inhabit the darkness. It's the only privacy they have. Once, their mother had lain between them, but not for many years now, not since they were grown girls and had walked with her body to the little cemetery on the hillside and watched her coffin being pushed into its marble slot as though being tucked into a drawer.

A dull yellow light is seeping through the shutters from the street lamps outside. It won't be daylight for another hour. Olimpia can dimly see the painted cherubs and wrought iron vines on the enamelled footboard – an identical, abbreviated version of the one behind her head. The bed is too high, the base sags and the mattress has long since worn into two lumpy pockets. But the furniture had come with the apartment above the shop – old Salvatore's marriage bed no doubt. Olimpia tries not to think of it. On the opposite wall there's a painted angel in a rococo frame – the colours are faded now and blurred with damp, but in daylight you can still see the blues and yellows and once-vivid greens that fill the background. In the foreground, the angel's improbably white gown has darkened to a dirty beige.

Olimpia slides her legs over the side of the bed towards the hard, terracotta tiles. Marina is awake now, blinking against the pillow. Neither of them say anything to each other. They have long since passed the need for language in the ordinary transactions of every day. Olimpia walks into the bathroom, moving slowly as if sleep-walking, to wash down to her waist in the bowl on the marble wash-stand that has to be filled with a jug from the tap. There's a shower, but it's rusted through, dripping cold water onto the tiles. It has never worked well, but they manage with a bowl, just as they did when they were children.

Olimpia's body is still heavy with sleep as she struggles into clothes that feel, this morning, like another woman's garments. Then she forces her spreading feet into the stiff black shoes with their velcro fastenings. Olimpia envies Marina her tiny feet – those long, narrow bones, each one like the foot of a bird.

Olimpia is small, barely five feet when she can stand erect; but she feels smaller, since her spine has begun to collapse in upon itself, curving her shoulders and tilting her head so that, unless she makes a great effort, her face is towards the ground. Nevertheless, *communque*, as they always say when they look at her, particularly men, who stare as if they are appraising an animal, *communque*, she is taller than her sister Marina.

When they were eight and nine years old they had been the same height, but then Marina had stopped growing and shortly afterwards, Olimpia too. Their mother, who was taller, said that it was because they had had to live on chestnuts during the war. Chestnut soup, chestnut *gnocchi*, chestnut flour, chestnuts raw and chestnuts roasted. Sometimes there was nothing else – maybe a few fronds of wild asparagus in the spring, or porcini mushrooms if you knew where to look in the autumn, sheep's cheese when the sheep had milk and before the soldiers shot the sheep.

When they are both dressed, the sisters make their way carefully down the marble steps to the *edicola* at the bottom of the street for a copy of *Il Terreno*, to read who has been born, who has died, another blood bath on the autostrada, another politician denying corruption. Today there's a photo of *Il Papa*, a benign figure in white, raising a trembling hand that looks too fragile for the papal ring he wears on his third finger. Olimpia can see his feet peeping out under the hem of his lace robe, but the black and white newsprint does not show the colour of the soft, red slippers they say he has made to order by Gucci. The caption beneath the photograph is undecipherable without her reading glasses. Olimpia puts the paper in her bag to read tonight over supper. It's a small treat she reserves for the long, dark evenings.

This morning, it's too cold to sit outside the bar, but inside it's hot and steamy. Matteo has seen them coming across the piazza and set out their usual table in the corner. Already there are two brioches on the counter, a *caffè corretto* for herself and a hot chocolate for Marina. Every morning

159

the same. Olimpia thinks their lives are like a clock, ticking precisely through the days and nights, round and round.

'How does it go, Matteo?'

'*Bene, abbastanza bene.*'

'Only well enough?' Olimpia gives a dry laugh. 'And how is Pia?'

'She is well.'

'And the *bambina*?'

'*Bellissima!*' He smiles at last.

'You must tell Pia to come and see us – we would like to see the baby.'

Lately Olimpia has begun to look in the baby carriages at the small closed faces and the tufts of hair. Little blanks, waiting to be stamped with their own personalities.

Under the dark mask of the coffee, she can feel the bitter kick of grappa on her tongue. Her heartbeat quickens, the café tables come into focus. Marina is bent over her chocolate, dipping her brioche like a child. Olimpia can see the white circle of hair on the crown of her head, like a monk's tonsure, where the dye is growing out, and wonders if her own looks the same. It seems such a waste of time to colour it now, but Marina says it is important to keep up appearances for the customers.

It's time to open for business. From the front of the shop, as she unlocks the shutters, Olimpia twists her body round to look up at the mountains. She can pick out the very fold of the rock, a line of darker green in the trees, where their village had been. Some parts of it had still been standing when they were last there, but that's a long time ago now. Once a year, in the autumn, they had made the pilgrimage, walking two or three hours up the mule track to the village. And then they would sit in the small piazza beside the carved trough that they had used for washing and bathing. It was fed by a spring that still welled through the rock into a cavern, under the roots of the gigantic Quercia tree that shaded the piazza now. It wasn't even a sapling when she was a girl, but on their last visit you could see its roots trailing down into the cistern. And every year, the walls of the houses tilted further towards the valley, and the roof tiles fell through the floors into terracotta dust, and bamboo and wild clematis grew over the olive terraces and the little vegetable gardens that had fed them all, before the war had taken the men away.

Olimpia can no longer make the pilgrimage because her sister is too frail, her heart too weak, so the shrine to the Madonna will be covered with weeds, the candles unlit, the flowers withered. When Olimpia wakes in the night it's this thought that prevents her from closing her eyes again. Though they light candles in the Duomo to the memory of their mother and father and their brothers, it's not the same.

For that Madonna, the Madonna of the Rock, was the one who had saved their lives, when the soldiers had come and their mother had prayed to the Madonna for help and they had gone into the cistern, holding on to the wall at the back, in the dark, and the water so cold their bones had cracked. But the soldiers had not found them, though one had stopped to drink and fill his water bottle there – he had not seen them, nor heard Marina's whimper of fear. The men had not been so fortunate. Their father and three brothers had been in the mountains with the partisans and only one of them had come back.

'*Salve Signora!*'

161

The voice belongs to the Milanese woman, Anastasia Segreto. She is taking her dog for its morning walk. Olimpia watches anxiously as it sniffs the door posts.

'*Basta*, Fidel!' Anastasia tugs on the lead. 'Don't even think of it!' Then she turns to Olimpia and smiles. 'Have you heard the news?'

'No. We don't switch the radio on in the mornings.'

'The Pope is going to resign! His health they say. What do you think?'

'The Pope to resign? *Madonna*! Are you sure it's true?'

'Oh yes. He's made a statement. It's very odd, though. Popes don't retire do they?'

Olimpia doesn't know what say. 'It's a very strange world we live in.'

Anastasia nods. 'But I must go - Fidel hasn't had his walk yet. *Ci vediamo Signora.*'

The shop smells of shoe leather and polish – an odour so heavy you can almost see it. The smell of rows of shoes set out on the shelves; two-tone brown and cream brogues in pigskin, thick-soled walking shoes, suede slip-ons to cushion painful toe joints, black leather lace-ups with stout heels and fringed tongues ready to accommodate the most awkward of feet. Shoes of the utmost respectability, beyond reproach.

Marina had once suggested that perhaps they might, perhaps they should, sell something a little more modern? But Olimpia had pointed out the folly of buying stock that would be out of fashion in a twelve month. And besides, how could they ever know what those beautiful young girls would like to wear – twittering like a flock of birds on their slender legs across the piazza, some of them wearing heels so high their bodies tilted forwards like trees in the wind?

'Stick to what you know!' she had said to Marina. It was only common sense. And what they know is how to pamper and comfort the feet of those who are no longer young.

The high ceiling of the shop is cool and dark. It is stained with decades of dust and insects and cigarette smoke. The walls are lined with shelves, and there's a wooden ladder to reach the top levels, as warped and bent with age as the bones of the sisters themselves. Neither Olimpia nor Marina venture further than the third step now. It irritates Olimpia that there are boxes of perfectly good shoes stranded on the upper shelves that will never be sold.

Olimpia goes outside to look at the window, where shoes line up in orderly rows, the men's segregated to the left – women's to the right. It has always been Marina's job to arrange them in little groups, balancing selected shoes on boxes draped with velvet, but it is several months since she has roused herself to do anything but tidy the gloves on the counter, exchanging summer for winter, and sometimes, when she feels particularly well, polishing the umbrella rack. A pair of rather dusty black suede court shoes with wine-glass heels sit, abandoned, on a pedestal at the back of the window. No one wears such things now; they are too unfashionable for the young, and too uncomfortable for the old.

A few months ago, Pia, the young Greek girl from the bar, had come in with some brightly coloured silk scarves she had printed herself and begged them to take a few, to hang in the window. If anyone bought one they could keep half the money. She was living with Anastasia Segreto, the Milanese, and had seemed very anxious. Olimpia had heard rumours that she was expecting Matteo's baby, so perhaps it was true. As she looked at the girl, at her pale face, her fragile wrists and thickening waist, the darkness in Pia's eyes had reminded Olimpia of someone else, and another child conceived out of wedlock. The memory was so strong she had to hold onto the edge of the counter for a moment. The moment had passed, but it left an acid taste in Olimpia's mouth.

She became aware that the girl was watching her with an expression of concern on her face. Olimpia had forced herself to smile and then to wonder aloud whether Pia realised that they shared the same name.

'My father always wanted to go to Greece, you know,' Olimpia had said to her as she fingered the silk, without knowing why she had begun chattering. 'That's why he gave us Greek names. He loved everything Greek. He had a book with all the pictures of the temples. And he knew all the stories. One of his uncles had been there, in the navy, after the first war, and he had brought back the book. My father could read. He was very clever.'

The connection between them was tenuous, but it was there. And so they had taken a few of the scarves and draped them over an old towel rail at the side of the display. The beautiful girls had stopped to look at them, pointing and laughing at the shoes in the window display – but they had come in to buy the scarves. To Olimpia's amazement they had sold them all in a week. She had kept one of the scarves for herself, a rich, celestial blue, hidden at the bottom of the drawer, to give to Marina as a

Christmas present.

When Pia came back, Olimpia had given her all the money – for the baby, she said, because by then it was obvious that she was carrying a child. 'Next time, we'll take half, if you can bring us some more.' But Pia had never come back. They said that Matteo had done the right thing by her, that they were living in an apartment owned by his father down at the marina. Olimpia hopes that she is happy.

At the back of the shop is the mirror, like a tall ghost in a carved chestnut-wood frame. At the top, the figure of Jesus sits, perched on a tangle of polished branches, with one arm across his chest and the other raised as if in admonition. Olimpia has trained herself not to look in the mirror as she passes, but sometimes she catches Marina sneaking a glance and once, when she came in suddenly through the door, she saw Marina preening her hair, which is still full and curly around her face, in the same style she has had since the war, when their mother had cut off their hair with a knife because there was no soap to wash it with.

It's time to switch on the electronic till. Olimpia misses the old one, with its manual keys and the reassuring ring when you entered the price. You had to press very firmly and deliberately – not like this one – it's so easy to catch the wrong number with the edge of a finger. But the bank said that they must have it for the *Carte di Credito*, even though all their customers pay in cash. When old Salvatore was alive, there had always been two prices – one for the window and one on the black – money that went into his pocket so that the government wouldn't tax it. But Marina wants to do everything by the rules – she's afraid that one day the *Guardia di Finanza* will draw up outside, their blue lights flashing, and rush inside to arrest them both and confiscate their account books. Pointless to argue that the *Guardia* have their diaries full with the factory owners, the tourist restaurants, the *Mafiosi*, and no time to spare for a shoe shop that sells no more than three or four pairs of shoes a week.

The shop seems bigger now than when they first came, and emptier. But there is always someone who comes in – out of curiosity, or gossip. Today it is their neighbour Giorgio, who is making a little *passagiata*. Since his wife died he roams the streets and the bars during the day. At night Olimpia can hear his television blaring out across the street, often late into the night, when he has fallen asleep in the chair. She has never been into his apartment, of course, but that is how she imagines it.

'*Mamma mia!*' he says, as he lowers himself down into one of the leather seats for customers, pausing half way down, propping himself with his stick. '*O dio!*'

Marina has retreated behind the counter and is doing something to the gloves.

'It's a struggle, Giorgio,' Olimpia says. 'And it doesn't get any easier.'

'No, by god!' He's rubbing his hands. 'You haven't lit the stove yet?'

Olimpia shakes her head. 'Not yet. We manage for as long as we can. Do you know what Mario charges for the logs now?'

'Matteo is getting one of those pellet things at the bar, you know. They burn clean, and the bags aren't heavy to carry.'

Olimpia grunts.

'Do you not have trouble with the mould? My apartment is terrible! My winter shoes were green with it when I took them out of the wardrobe. And the ceiling's quite black in places with the spores. I've told the landlord, but he won't do a thing.'

Olimpia sniffs the air, as if checking for mould, but it smells as it always does. 'We're quite dry here, thank god.' Then after a pause she says. 'Someone told me that the Pope is going to retire. Is that a joke do you think?'

'Matteo told me when I went into the bar for my coffee. It's in the papers.'

'I couldn't believe it! Popes don't retire.'

'Well, why shouldn't he? He's an old man and he's sick. How can he do the job if he's ill?' Then he grins. 'Maybe this time we get an Italian!'

Giorgio is already heaving himself out of the seat again with one hand braced on the wooden armrest. He gives a sharp intake of breath, as if he has a spasm of pain, as he straightens up. 'It's cruel,' he says. 'But what can one expect? At my age. And after hammering the shit out of the marble for so many years.' He's looking at his hand, held out in front of him – the swollen joints, the missing digit from his second finger. 'I was a good *artigiano*, anyway – better than most of the *stranieri* who call themselves sculptors nowadays. Have you seen what they have put in the piazza this week?' Giorgio waves his stick towards the door. 'I go sometimes to look at the little *pietà* in Sant' Agostino and I feel better you know. If it makes people feel better when they look at it, then it's been worth it. Don't you think?'

Olimpia doesn't agree, but she nods. What was the point of wasting your body over things? But maybe, marble being more durable than shoe leather . . . though she's not convinced.

Giorgio is at the door. 'Now I must go, because I'm meeting Luca in the piazza for a game of *Briscola* – I've beaten him three times this week already. He's not what he was. *Madonna*! At least I still have my faculties.' He stands for a moment looking round. 'You should give all this up, you know, Olimpia. It's too hard.'

'But what would we do all day, Giorgio?'

'Enjoy your time a little – soon it will be too late for all of us. The Pope is a wise man.' He doesn't expect an answer, and shuffles out towards the steps. '*Ci vediamo, signore. A domani!*'

Tomorrow. Olimpia suddenly has a vision of all the tomorrows in front of her, exactly like today, repeating into infinity.

Olimpia has never once, in all the years that they have been here, told Marina how much she hates shoes – their yawning mouths, protruding tongues, the laces that remind her of the corsets they had to wear when they were young. She has never told how much the smell of leather, of tanning chemicals and dead beasts, makes her nauseous. And the white boxes like little coffins where the shoes lie together, facing each other, like lovers. And how she dreams sometimes of disembodied feet laced into shoes of vicious colours, tip-tapping their sinister dances up the stairs, through the *sala* into her bedroom, right up to the bed, before she manages to wake.

But how could she have refused, when Didi sent the money from America and the letter, saying that he had heard that old Salvatore was giving up the shop and he thought that it would provide for his sisters? And he would send the rent every month until they were making money. A home for Marina, a roof, a way of putting bread on the table, and Marina looking at her with those dark, blank eyes, afraid of a shadow, afraid to look at a man, unable to work, or even face going out into the street alone.

And it is at this moment that Olimpia feels a tremor under her feet, as if the ground is shifting. Then a shiver seems to run across the floor and the shelves begin to shake and rattle. At the moment of greatest intensity, when the light fittings are swinging and the shoe boxes begin to topple from the shelving, suddenly the mirror falls, as if hurled down, like a sign or a revelation. Where the mirror had been on the wall is a naked patch of stucco, cracked and peeling, in a strange reddish colour, as though the wall had bled into the plaster.

Marina is screeching, clutching the counter and looking at the bright shards of glass on the floor, the splinters of reflection, ceiling, shelves, and shoes, scattered across the marble. And among them is the carved Jesus from the pediment. Olimpia has never noticed that he is holding up his hand in the same gesture as *Il Papa* in this morning's photograph.

When they have swept the shards into a plastic bin, it's time for Olimpia to go to Rosa's for the tordelli and one of her good sauces ladled into a plastic box. With plenty of bread, if you're careful, it's possible to make it last two days. This evening, Marina comes with her, not wanting to be alone in case there's another tremor.

The distance across the piazza seems much further tonight. And it's almost empty. The crazy English musician has gone south for the winter, but sour-faced Taj, in his red robes and Tibetan hat, is crouched on the steps of the Bank of Rapallo, setting out his possessions and his instruments, ready for the evening *passaggiata*. Thank God they have taken his dog away. Poor, starving thing. If it hadn't been for the tourists feeding it . . .

'What a *terremoto!*' Rosa says. 'It was the worst for years. I could see the bell swinging and swinging in the campanile, and I was waiting for it to ring, the way it did in 1968, but, you know, it didn't! That was extraordinary.'

'The mirror fell down. *Mamma mia*, what a mess!' Olimpia says.

'The big one in the shop?' Rosa wheezes as she shovels the pasta onto a cardboard tray. Rosa has eaten too many of her own tordelli. 'You know it belonged to old Salvatore's wife? Her mother worked for the priest out at Pieve. I think she got it when he died.'

She tucks the tray into a paper bag, gives the neck of the bag a quick twist and puts it down on the counter. 'I'll bet it's seen some things, that mirror. He was an old scoundrel! Ask Giorgio and his brother – they repaired the font in the church and they were never paid.'

As Rosa puts the money into the plastic box she keeps under the till she looks up and says, 'It's a sign, you know.'

'A sign?'

'The *terremoto*. On the day that the Pope has told us that he will no longer be pope. Think of it, Olimpia – there will be two popes!' Rosa shudders. 'It's a sign!'

Later, when they are getting into bed, Marina pauses suddenly, with her leg already raised towards the mattress.

'Do you remember Pavel?' she asks. Her rarely-used voice is quiet and apologetic.

Olimpia says nothing. It's a long time since

170

anyone has mentioned Pavel, the man they had called the Turkoman and sometimes 'Pavel the *Mussulman*', who had lived in a hut outside the village after the war with his flock of sheep and who had given them ricotta – holding out the dish with a smile and a few words of Italian. As soon as Marina had said Pavel's name, his face had sprung up as if in sunshine. His mouth was laughing, but his eyes were black with all the things he had seen. And behind him, she had glimpsed the others. All those beautiful, cruel boys. What had it been about? What had it meant? She feels sick with loss.

In the darkness she can hear Giorgio's television across the street. An advertising jingle for yogurt. And she can see the Pope's red shoes, marching, marching, hundreds of pairs of them to the sound of the music.

11

After Michelangelo

When the last wife left, she took the computer and the dog. Martin finds that it's the dog he misses most. At the moment he's feeding pieces of focaccia and mortadella to Beni, who is snuffling them up with his bulldog snout, crouching patiently under a nearby chair, waiting for Enzo to take him home.

It's market day. From his table at the corner of the piazza Martin can observe the people strolling in from the side-streets. Purposeful country women come from the direction of the bus stop, square shouldered and stout, clutching shopping bags and wearing quilted waistcoats in anticipation of the coolness of November. In an hour they will come lurching back with bags weighed down by vegetables, fruit, cheese and saucepans as well as carrier bags of woolen jumpers and floral pyjamas.

Anastasia appears, looking elegant in black, towing Fidel who growls aggressively at Beni. 'May I?' she asks, in English, indicating the empty seat, although she knows he isn't going to refuse. She folds herself into the chair, turning it round a little so that she can still see the piazza and gives a long sigh.

'I like the winter, when the tourists have gone and we can be comfortable among ourselves again.'

Martin thinks she's looking better; less anxious. 'How's your lodger?'

'Very nice! I didn't think I could get on with a Korean woman. She speaks very little Italian you know. But she's so clean and polite and quiet. Sometimes I forget I have someone in the apartment at all!'

Martin raises his arm and shouts for Matteo who's standing in the doorway looking in the opposite direction. 'Lazy bastard. You never get a smile out of him and when you want a drink he's hiding at the back of the bar. Do you know what he did yesterday?'

Anastasia shakes her head.

'Brought my drink and then he bangs down a till receipt on the table and waits for the money up front as if I was a bloody tourist.'

The Polish women are laughing and chattering at one of the other tables – plump blondes, drinking Aperol spritz and displaying their purchases to each other. One of them is holding up a cashmere jumper she's just bought from the twenty euro stall – bright red with tiny crystals sewn around the neck and down the front. It's quite hideous, but her friends admire it. They're chattering in their own language and one of them has a laugh like a mocking bird. Martin tries not to listen.

'I like them, you know,' Anastasia says, smiling at his expression. 'They're always so cheerful.'

'I just wish they weren't so bloody noisy. What do they do all day?'

'They work as maids in the big holiday houses and once I saw one of them pushing an elderly woman around the piazza in a wheelchair, so I think they must sometimes also work as *badante*.'

Matteo comes and stands beside the table with his

order pad.

'How is Pia?' Anastasia asks, 'and the *bambina*?'

Matteo's facial expression remains the same. 'They are okay.' He shrugs. 'The baby cries a lot.'

'They always do. It gets better.'

Matteo looks unconvinced. His eyes look as if he hasn't slept. Martin orders another coffee with a grappa chaser and Anastasia orders a *spuma bionda*.

'I bought myself a bag in the market,' she says by way of explanation. 'So I have to do penance until Miko pays the rent on Friday. I don't know where the money goes – this place gets more expensive every day.' She rolls another thin wrap of Golden Virginia.

Martin nods agreement. Fidel is making love to his leg under the table. 'When I first came here a glass of wine was one euro – now it's three fifty. And coffee is two.'

Anastasia lights the roll-up and gives a flick of her head to toss her hair back. 'Soon there will only be German tourists and Milanese weekenders. I call them the art tourists.'

Martin laughs derisively. 'There'll be nothing for them to see shortly. All the artists are leaving – the rents are just too high. It seems crazy when you think that people come here because of us, and the tourists are driving us out.'

'Is it as bad as that?'

'The rents are ridiculous. And more and more marble studios are closing – the *artigiani* are all going to Carrara. Give it a year or two and this place will be just a smart shopping destination. It's enough to make you puke.'

'I remember when I was a girl, sitting here and it

was all *artigiani* and artists – a few writers. They would sit every evening in the bar until nine o'clock – sometimes later. My father knew everyone. There was such a good atmosphere. Now . . .' Anastasia shrugs and spreads her hands wide in a gesture of contempt.

'What will you do?'

'In a few years I am "*in pensione*" and then it will be okay. I don't have to pay rent for the apartment, thank God! And you?'

Martin pulls a face. 'I might have to go back to England. At least there I can get grants and benefits, enough to scrape a living – some teaching maybe. The government will pay my rent. But I won't be able to carve marble there.'

It's not a good thought – for fifteen years this has been Martin's life – the piazza, the ridge of broken marble mountains against the skyline, the sea lapping the periphery of the town, the textures and colours of the stone stacked in the marble yards scattered among the streets, just waiting for someone to shape, to scour and polish. There's a piece of alabaster he's coveting in an abandoned yard just behind the Duomo, in a shed half hidden under brambles and wild clematis. He knows it will carve soft and polish to a transparent sheen. He has an idea for a kind of mask, a head and shoulders maybe, with translucent breasts . . .

A high-pitched electronic scream interrupts his thoughts. The mobile resuscitation unit is ploughing through the market with a police escort – the crowds part in front of it and gather again behind to watch its progress.

'*O Dio!*' Anastasia shudders. 'How I hate those things!'

Martin watches to see where the ambulance will

stop, where the angel of death has perched. Perhaps it can be startled into flight by the howling siren? The wailing sound adds to Martin's feeling of depression.

It has stopped near the shoe shop, blocking the entrance to the narrow street. One of the Polish women crosses herself.

'Not one of the sisters,' Anastasia says. 'Oh, I do hope not.'

'The Weird Sisters.' Martin can't resist. '*I Nani.*'

Anastasia gives him a *Look*.

Across the piazza, Martin can see that Stefania is writing the day's specials on the board outside the pizzeria. She does it deliberately, wetting her finger to erase her mistakes and then carefully outlining a new word. The *antipasti* are in yellow chalk, *primi* in white, *secondi* in blue and the *dolce* suitably pink. The new owner comes out wiping the pizza flour from his hands with his apron and looks over her shoulder as if inspecting the work. He says something and she gives a quick, submissive nod of the head. She looks like a girl of sixteen against his fourteen stone of muscle and bone. His head is shaved, so Martin suspects he's going bald. They are vain, these Italian men.

'What happened to Franco?' Anastasia asks, following the direction of his gaze. 'Have you heard anything?'

'I helped him to get a job in some pizza place in London. A friend of a friend. But I think I'll live to regret it. I never told them about his drinking.' Martin had felt guilty about all those convivial evenings in the bar watching Franco's tipsy cabaret, the consumption of free grappa and *biscotti*.

'I haven't been inside the pizzeria since he left,' Anastasia says, 'but someone told me that his flags and souvenirs, the pictures of Mick Jagger and the Queen have all disappeared and now it looks just like any other pizza place. Boring.'

As they watch, Stefania turns to look around the piazza for a moment. She seems sad – there's a kind of stillness about her, a lack of animation. Martin wonders if she really is better off without Franco.

'Last week I went up to Monticolegno for a walk,' he says.

'You went to his house?'

Martin had walked past it out of curiosity, but the house was closed up – the shutters fixed and the door padlocked. 'The *barista* in the little café told me that Stefania's moved back in with her mother. "Half a bottle of grappa every day before he went to the piazza," the man said, "and then, what he drank while he worked." How could she stand it? No one can live like that.'

Anastasia sighs. 'What does one do with all the Francos in this world?'

The blue light on top of the ambulance is still flashing.

The lunchtime *pausa* is over and Martin knows he must go and brave the dragon at the Studio Bertolozzi. It takes a big ego to do good work, in Martin's opinion. You have to have balls and there are women here who have more balls than any man Martin has ever met. Shira is one of them – working in a man's world, an Italian man's world at that, has hardened her. Martin thinks that her two years national service in the Israeli Defence Force must also have been a good grounding. She's as tough as they come, and probably a dyke, Martin assumes, since she doesn't seem to find men attractive. *Rompe coglioni*, they say here. A ball breaker.

'You still owe me for the stone,' Shira says, looking him straight in the eye.

It puts Martin on the defensive. 'I can't pay you till I sell the sculpture. But Carla has someone interested, or so she says.'

'Oh, Carla!' Shira gives a derisive toss of the head. 'And even if she sells it, you could wait months for the money. She's a slow payer.'

That's true, but credit never used to be a problem. Martin has always worked in arrears, getting the stone from Shira, and paying her as soon as the finished object was sold. What's changed?

'Anyway,' Shira's saying, 'I don't have room for you at the moment. The studio's full.'

'Tourists!' Martin says. 'People who've retired on full pensions and think they can now afford to be to be artistic. What's the fucking point!'

'The fucking point is money,' Shira says. 'You know how many studios have gone out of business in the last year?'

'Okay. Okay. I'll find somewhere else.'

Shira's face softens, just a fraction. 'Sorry, Martin.' He shrugs.

'Are you going to the *Lizzatura* on Sunday?'

'What's that?'

'Shame Martin! Where have you been? It's the re-enactment of the way they used to bring the marble blocks down from the quarries with pulleys and wooden rollers instead of trucks. Haven't you seen the posters?'

Martin has a vague memory of some of the *artigiani* talking about it but it hadn't seemed very relevant.

'You should go.' Shira says. 'It's going to be quite

179

an event.'

'Shira's right, you ought to go,' Trine says in the bar after work. 'It's not just a historic thing, it's a kind of homage to all those men who risked their lives to get the marble out.'

Martin's on his third Campari. 'I haven't any transport so I don't know how the hell she thought I was going to get there. I need a lift.' He glances at Rose Umber. Rose has a moped, and she's going up on it.

She looks at Martin dubiously over her café latte. 'Don't be offended, but I don't honestly think it would carry both of us uphill. Anyway, I'm taking Trine.'

'Why don't you get the special bus?' Trine suggests. 'It's leaving from the studio about nine in the morning. Some of the old *artigiani* are going up on that.'

'I'll think about it.'

'There's a rumour there's going to be trouble,' Rose says. 'You know there's a lot of bad feeling about the amount of quarrying going on?'

'They can't blame us,' Trine says. 'There are very few sculptors here now. It's not us using all that marble.'

Rose nods a violent agreement. 'Shira was saying that ever since they got the diamond blades in the quarries, they've been shovelling the stuff out for bathroom tiles and kitchen surfaces and god knows what else. Some of it's ground down for toothpaste, apparently. The mountains are disappearing at a fantastic rate. There are some photos on the internet.'

The staircase smells of mildew. Damp November when the mould spreads over the walls and ceilings like eczema and even gets into the wardrobe. Martin's jacket had been quite green around the collar and cuffs when he took it out last night.

It's a long way up to the top floor and the thick chestnut door to the two-room roof apartment he's borrowing from Renee Lange, a German sculptor who's gone home for the winter.

'Don't turn the thermostat above sixteen,' she'd said to him before she left, 'it's very expensive.' Martin spins the dial to twenty and hears the boiler fire up in the hallway.

It's very small. Only a tiny kitchen, with a circular table and chairs squeezed up against the units, and next door a tiny bedroom with a shower cubicle and loo in the corner. The bed looks very inviting.

There's a piece of pecorino cheese and some prosciuto in the fridge, but Martin decides he's no longer hungry. There's a little bit of coffee in the tin. Enough for his breakfast. Martin puts it back on the surface next to the espresso pot. It's too late for coffee.

Martin sits on the edge of the bed. He feels tired, but not weary enough, or drunk enough, to sleep. He's afraid of the dreams that materialise out of the shadowy corners of the room, filling the darkness with an anxiety as tangible as smoke. There is one dream in particular that he has never told anyone about. In the dream he was in a cave – perhaps a marble cavern – with long stalactites hanging from the ceiling everywhere. They were very strange – like shrouded figures wrapped in bandages. And then he'd walked into another cave and there were marble benches with shapes in white laid out on them being prepared to be hung up. Martin looked at one of them closely and through all the bandages he'd recognised his father. This dream has recurred several times and he always wakes up sweating under the weight of the darkness, hardly able to breathe.

He takes the mail, which he had retrieved from the box on the way up, out of his pocket. There's a note from Carla Falcone that simply says 'Ring me!' with a mobile number scribbled underneath. Martin wonders if there's a problem with the sale of his sculpture. Surely not? The gay American guy had taken an immediate liking to his marble sculpture of buttocks and thighs – a copy of the lower torso of one of the Kouros in the museum in Athens. The Greeks had known what they were doing – all this fuss about Michelangelo – the Greeks had done it all centuries before he came along. There is a kind of rapture in their lines that sings – Martin surprises himself with this thought – like a true note – perfect pitch. Michelangelo had got near it, but never quite on the note.

And another thought – much bleaker – follows that one. If Michelangelo Buonarotti was, at best, close – what is Martin himself? The answer to that isn't one that Martin wants to consider.

In the spindly antique bedside cabinet there's a bottle of grappa that still has a couple of inches in the bottom. '*Ciao, Amico!*' Martin says as he holds it up to the light. The sweetest dreams are no dreams at all.

Martin has seen the old photographs in the museum – the intricate cat's-cradle of hawsers and tree trunks and wedges; the men standing with long poles, shirts open and faces squinting up at the sun under their broad-brimmed hats.

It doesn't look quite like that today. The rain has been falling all night and the marble cobbles are slippery underfoot as Martin gets off the bus with the others. He recognises Marcone, the foreman from the quarry, and there's the old midwife, Nonna, whose father – a winchman – had been crushed by a shifting block of marble. Then there's the two old *artigiani* Giorgio and Luca whose grandfather had been one of the wiremen at the quarry. The men taking part are all young – mostly men from the marble yards and apprentices from the studios. Pierluigi, the *artigiano* from Shira's studio is already there, grasping a cable.

The hillside down from the quarry road is very steep – a scree of quarry waste, but that is the route the men are proposing to take. The observers have all gathered on the side of the road where the bus has dropped them. Rose and Trine are at the back of the crowd. The men are standing looking down at the wet marble scree.

'It will go fast,' Giorgio says. 'Maybe a little too fast.'

The block of marble, about three metres by two, weighs nearly eighteen tons. It's trussed in hawsers like a Christmas parcel. The ends are wound around a massive tree trunk wedged in the rock above. A marble block on a trolley is being used as a counter-weight on the opposite slope.

The men at the front are there to place the wooden rollers, running from front to back. The winchman sits above the pulleys and shouts orders, the hawsers slacken and tighten, creaking through the pulley wheels as the sled crunches and groans across the rollers. Sweat is pouring off even the youngest of the men, although the temperature is only about eight degrees.

Down below, Martin can see the olive groves as a patchwork of green and silver and orange, where the

183

nets have been slung between the trees to catch the falling olives. When the men pause to rest you can hear the tap and rattle of bamboo canes in the branches.

In the temporary silences it's also possible to hear another bus scrunching up the quarry track, its engine straining in low gear. Everyone turns to look as it pulls up behind their own and people begin to pour out and surge towards the *Lizzatura*. At first Martin thinks they're simply tourists and then realises with amazement that they're carrying placards with 'Hands off the Alpi Apuane', and similar slogans on them. There's a banner unfurling that reads 'Stop Stealing Our Mountains'.

'It's the Greens,' Martin hears someone say. 'They've been petitioning the state governor to stop the quarrying.'

One of the protestors has produced a megaphone and begins to shout through it, but the echo from the walls of the quarry makes it impossible for Martin to understand what he's saying.

Some of the *artigiani* leave their positions to confront the protestors – there's some pushing and shoving in the crowd. Martin can hear one of the old men swearing. Then, out of the corner of his eye, Martin sees someone darting round the perimeter of the group – a quick, slight figure whose face is hidden with a scarf, heading quickly for the sledge. Martin sees him or her jump up onto the block and there's the flash of a blade as they bend towards the ropes.

'Hey!' Martin yells. 'You can't do that!'

He turns to run down the slope towards the saboteur. 'Down here!' he shouts to the others. '*Giu! Subito!*' He can hear the rattle of stones as feet begin to run down behind him.

Just as he reaches the sledge and tries to stop, grasping the corner of the marble to balance himself, his feet slide from under him on the rain-soaked scree and then he is falling, falling, looking back at the marble block above him and the jagged, quarried-out summit of the mountain behind it framed against the grey sky.

When Martin opens his eyes again he's puzzled to see a vista of white and blue and the glare of fluorescent lights. He's aware that he has the worst hangover in the world – the full-on Iron Helmet. His mouth feels dry and there's a strange, chemical smell that reminds him of hospitals. One of his legs is numb.

Shira is looking down at him. She seems very angry.

'You'd better come and stay at my place for a while,' she says. 'You aren't going to make the fourth floor.'

12

The Feast of Santa Lucia

'Suffering. The harshness of living
and what we know of loving. All
the unsayable things. But afterwards
under the dumb stars
all we are left with is words . . .'
Rilke, Duino Elegies, No 9.

It's the feast of Santa Lucia, the patron saint of light, a celebration of the earth turning once more towards the sun.
Someone has tied a helium balloon to the bronze horse
rearing on its plinth in the centre of the square. The balloon is lit from within and glows above the Duomo like a
perigee moon.

You can hear singing – the echo of voices from
somewhere on the other side of the piazza. Trine and Rose
Umber have persuaded two of the beautiful girls, Mariella
and Angelina, to join them in singing the traditional Santa
Lucia anthem around the square. Trine has taught them
the Danish tune and translated the words into Italian.
Rose, who used to sing in a choir, takes the alto line and
Trine lifts a fine descant over the tune, which wobbles
occasionally as the two Italian girls lose their way in the

unfamiliar music.

They are all dressed in white robes made from sheets, tied at the waist with silver tinsel. They have lighted candles on their heads and move like flaming ghosts around the piazza. Rose and Trine have made garlands from wire and tinsel to hold the four candles they are wearing like crowns. They have had to cover their hair with aluminium cooking foil to protect it from the melting wax. After the rehearsal last night, Mariella had to iron her hair and then wash and tooth-comb it to remove the drips.

Outside the Bar di Pietro, Matteo and Eva are setting out glasses on a long table. Tonight is the opening of Carla Falcone's exhibition '*Omaggio di Michelangelo*'. Matteo is stacking bottles of prosecco in a dustbin full of ice ready for the influx of customers they expect once the gallery reception is over. Enzo comes out to see what they are doing, but he doesn't speak to Eva. He rarely does these days. Now that he's campaigning to become *Sindaco* he only has time to talk to important people. Eva looks un-happy. Two days ago Enzo's wife Hilaria had come into the kitchen where Eva was slicing oranges and told her that there was a good job going at a cocktail bar in Viareggio, owned by a friend of hers.

'It's better pay,' Hilaria had said. 'Just talk to Stefano and tell him I sent you.'

Eva hasn't gone yet, but she knows she must. There's a new barman, Fabrizio, who is going to replace Matteo. He's been here a week and already he's telling her what to do. And there is also Simona, doing some of Pia's shifts and just waiting to be given Eva's job. She's slow and clumsy, but she doesn't flinch when Enzo shouts at her. Since she was awarded her compensation by the court, Simona has seemed invincible. Whenever things go badly she shrugs her shoulders and says: 'When the old man dies, I will not have to do this!'

Babacar is standing on the corner of the piazza waiting for passing trade. Winter is difficult, without the tourists, and this summer there have been fewer of them than the previous year. Even the bars are complaining that trade is slow and the customers spend less. It is the fault of *la crisi*.

But Babacar has a caravan now, given by Brother Hermes, and there will be room for his wife and children, when he can save enough to bring them. Brother Hermes is going to help him with the papers. In a few more months he can apply to become a legal resident with proper permits and even a bank account. Maybe his dream of Europe will come true after all

The *straniero* sculptor goes past without looking at him, swinging his crutches in rhythm – dot two, carry one – his leg in a black velcro support. He had narrowly escaped death, they said. Babacar watches him stop outside the shoe shop and look up at the windows of the apartment. The shutters are down but, in the window above, there is a faint light.

Babacar feels sad. He had liked the Signora Olimpia and now she is dead, collapsing on the floor of the shop one morning – a blow to the heart, they had said – and now she is gone. He is still wearing the shoes she had given him and he misses her kindness, the little jokes they had shared. The other sister has not been seen since the funeral, when Babacar had watched her being helped

189

into a car by someone from the Croce Verde. There were, apparently, no other relatives.

Inside the Gallery Falcone, Anastasia is guarding the catalogues for Carla and greeting the arrivals. Behind her the room gleams with marble and bronze and other strange stone and metal installations. Martin Soulby has contributed a female torso carved in alabaster with translucent breasts. Anastasia thinks that everything he carves seems to be about sex – phalluses and buttocks. Once it was a giant clam-like object that reminded her of a vagina.

But Anastasia likes Rose's contribution, carved from pelagic limestone, with the fossil forms of sea creatures still in it. The sculpture is abstract, with flowing lines that resemble water, or the long tresses of a mermaid. The label says that it is 'Creation: The Fifth Day'.

Anastasia's Korean lodger has made an installation – a box that contains a letter in old Italian handwriting, a piece of broken white marble, a dusty bottle of wine with a handwritten label and some old tattered lire held down with a chisel. Apparently it's a reference to Michelangelo's time in Tuscany, when he worked for the Medici and lodged in the piazza writing letters complaining about the weather, the quality of the wine, and the amount he was being paid.

Some of the exhibits are much harder to understand. In one corner a spider mesh of silver wire hangs from the ceiling, lit from below, creating holograms of light on the ceiling as it sways to and fro in the draught created by the circulating guests. What that has to do with Michelangelo Anastasia doesn't know, 'But then,' she says to Mari-Elena, Matteo's mother, 'I'm only a simple soul – what do I know about art?'

'More than some of these people, I think,' Mari-Elena says, with a scornful gesture.

Mari-Elena has come for the baptism of Elena Christiana Olimpia, named for her grandmothers and, at the last moment, for her benefactress, Olimpia. Because, miraculously, the old woman has left her share of the shoe shop to the *bambina*. In the letter she left with the *Avvocato* she had said that it was because she and Pia shared the same name and, because she had no children of her own, would like the property to go to the offspring of her Greek namesake. The other sister, Marina, is to move into a *Casa di Riposa* and allow Matteo and Pia to live in the apartment and run the shop as they please.

'She hasn't made anything legal,' Mari-Elena says confidentially to Anastasia, 'but she's told them that she also intends to leave her share of the shop to the baby.'

Anastasia thinks how quickly fortunes can change. Your life can flick from comedy to tragedy and back as casually as the breeze turning the pages of a book.

There's the sound of singing in the street and then girls giggling; the smell of newly extinguished candles. Rose and Trine and two of the beautiful girls have arrived, still in their white robes with candle wax congealing on their shoulders.

Rose is avoiding Pierluigi. It's not that there is any real awkwardness – more a sense of embarrassment. She and Trine are getting along so well together these days. It's so much less complicated with a woman. Rose thinks that her parents would be horrified.

Pierluigi has come with a very glamorous older

woman. She looks slightly familiar and it takes Rose several minutes before she remembers the Swiss woman who had come to the studio in August, the one whose husband was in advertising.

'Hello,' Rose says, in French, as the woman pauses beside her sculpture. 'Didn't you come to the studio, a few months ago?'

'I did.' The woman smiles and holds out her hand. 'Frida. It feels good to be back.'

'What are you doing here?' Rose wonders whether the question is too blunt to be polite, but Frida doesn't seem put out.

'That's a long story. I'm studying at the film school in Geneva and I've come here to make a project.'

'Oh?'

'I'm going to put four cameras in the piazza and let them record everything for four weeks and then edit it down into a kind of narrative. It's called, 'Real Lives: Real Time'.'

Rose thinks it sounds rather pretentious, but she doesn't say so. 'Is your husband here with you?'

Frida's expression changes. She pulls a face and shakes her head. 'I left him.'

This is true, but not true. Frida had left him in the hotel and gone to Florence, but after three weeks she'd had a phone call from her daughter. Carl had suffered a heart attack and was in a Zurich hospital. Could she please come home? So Frida had gone. But she had stayed for only a month. Enough time to know that he would live, that he was having an affair with his assistant Jana, and that she wanted a divorce. So now Frida has an apartment in Geneva, a generous allowance, and a place at the academy of

192

arts to re-train for a future of her own.

Sometimes she thinks that the life she dreams of is only a mirage. When she comes back to the apartment alone, it seems very empty. And her daughter, whom she had hoped might be sympathetic, is angry and has grown much closer to her father.

'How could you leave him when he was ill?' she had asked.

In those moments, Frida feels the trap closing over her again. But she can see that Carl has lost a lot of weight since his bypass and Jana makes him laugh and is already telling him he must work less hours and she has enrolled him in a gym.

'We weren't good for each other,' she tells her daughter. 'We brought out the worst in each other. I was too weak and he was too strong. I gave in to him to have a peaceful life, but then it was no life at all.'

Her daughter isn't convinced. 'I don't want my parents in two different places! And I hate that scheming bitch Jana. My god, she's only a few years older than me! Before you know it she'll be taking over the company, and the house and everything.'

Your inheritance, Frida thinks. But it is for her daughter to learn that you must make a life for yourself – a life that depends on someone else is a second-hand life. No life at all.

Now Frida is looking at Pierluigi. They had made love this afternoon in the hotel with more care, but much less satisfaction than the first time, almost as if it was something that had to be got over before they could move on. He is her 'transitional man' she realises, a useful sticking plaster for the ego before she looks for something more solid and lasting. Pierluigi is already eyeing Angelina, with her white bed-sheet slipping off her shoulder and candle wax in her shoulder-length curls. She has a wide, muscular mouth, curved into a smile that is fixed on him and he is bending forward as if he really wants to hear what she's saying.

Anastasia watches Pia arrive with the baby accompanied by Stefania. Brother Hermes comes up to talk to them and Pia takes the baby out of the pram and gives her to him to hold. Anastasia is watching Hermes' face, the way his eyes change and his mouth twists as he rocks the baby and touches her cheek with his finger.

'They say he has a woman in Solaio,' a familiar voice says in her ear.

'Martin!' Anastasia says. 'You are an old gossip. You should be glad he is normal. These days it is hard to know.'

Martin grins. He is propping himself up on his crutches, his leg still encased in a black velcro support boot.

'How is it going?' Anastasia asks.

'It's a bugger,' he says. 'You can't carry a glass and walk at the same time. And I have to live with the dragon,' he adds, nodding towards Shira at the other side of the room in conversation with Carla Falcone.

Anastasia laughs. 'What are you doing for Christmas and New Year?'

'Back to England. I've got a check up at the hospital on Tuesday and then I can leave.'

'And will you be back?'

He sighs. 'Who knows. Depends if I can sell this.' He indicates the alabaster. 'At least I've got somewhere to live over there.'

'Where are you going?'

'I have a daughter by my first marriage and she's invited me to stay until I'm fully fit. I don't know whether I'll come back. It's become too difficult to sell things here.' He looks around with obvious regret. He waves a hand towards the old *artigiani* Giorgio and Luca standing on the other side of the room. 'Now they were the real thing. All that skill in their hands. They represent what's been lost.'

'Nothing stays the same,' Anastasia says. 'Everything changes.'

Giorgio and Luca are standing awkwardly in front of Trine's sculpture. Giorgio is wondering why they have come. The girl in the studio – the one who looks like an *artigiano* and wields a chisel like a man – had been very persuasive in the bar last night. But Giorgio feels uncomfortable and knows that Luca does too. They don't belong here among these people – people who once would have employed them to correct their mistakes, or even to make the sculpture for them, working from a small macquette or a drawing.

'*Madonna!*' Luca is saying, bending down to examine the object closely. It is an abstract, twisting shape that seems to have no form or meaning. 'How can this be the "*Anima di Davide*"? What does this have to do with either David or the soul?'

It is strange to look at these marble objects, most of them made by such amateurs, and know that the world that you have belonged to all your life has vanished.

'It has a very nice finish, though,' Luca goes on, running a hand over the smooth Carrara marble, reflecting the light like the moon on water. He's squinting to check

195

that the spiral lines flow properly without dips or kinks. 'Like silk.'

But Giorgio is not convinced. 'It's all bullshit, Luca. All of it.' He's trying not to look at a copy of the Hand of David done by one of the young sculptors from Studio Marcone. It makes him wince. 'Let's go and get an *aperitivo*.'

The girls have been persuaded to sing again and they form a tableau in the centre of the room. Carla won't let them light the candles in the gallery. As they begin to sing, there's a little disturbance by the door and Nonna comes in, leaning on a stick, accompanied by two of the Albanian boys, Nico and Zamir. They pause beside Anastasia as they enter.

Clara looks very frail. She has a transparent look as though already partly in the other world. Her face is tipped to one side as she listens to the singing. Anastasia can hear her murmuring 'Beautiful. Beautiful.'

'What happened with the pigeons,' Anastasia asks as she hands over a catalogue. She still feels guilty about signing the *denuncia*.

'Ah,' Nonna says, 'they have all flown.' She looks as if she might weep. 'The *comune* came round and they put the netting all round the loggia so that they can't come in and a man came and cleaned up everything – they smashed the eggs and swept it all up into a bin. The poor things.'

Nico says something Anastasia doesn't catch. Nonna pats his arm.

'The boys have made a *piccionaia* in the caravan park, in the loft of the old studio, you know. And they have invited the birds to come there. It's too far for me to walk, but

I like to think of them there. I give the boys the food for them.'

Anastasia smiles at Nico and he smiles back, exchanging a rather uncomfortable look with Zamir. Anastasia thinks their motives are probably not as pure as Nonna would like to believe. It is illegal to catch little birds now, but in the country villages they still roast thrushes and blackbirds on the spit. Roast pigeon is a delicacy, as are pigeon's eggs. Nonna obviously hasn't thought of that. Perhaps just as well.

Across the room Pia is standing with Stefania and Hermes and Mari-Elena. Soon it will be another year, Pia thinks, but this time she is filled with optimism as she takes the baby from Brother Hermes. Matteo has even talked about a wedding in the spring. Sometimes, cynically, Pia wonders whether he is motivated by the thought of the property that has been left to his little daughter, and the prospect of being free of his father. But she has such plans; the dresses she will make, the fabric she can create. The name above the door. Casa Pia. She fantasises about sitting in the shop on quiet afternoons with Elena playing on the floor, while she twists silver wire and coloured beads into bracelets and earrings. And all the beautiful girls in the piazza will be wearing them for the *passeggiata*.

'I have to go to work now,' Stefania says, touching her arm. '*In bocca al lupo*! I hope it all goes well for you.'

'And for you,' Pia says. 'I hope next year is better.'

Stefania pulls a face. 'It could not be worse, I think. You know Franco is coming back?'

'No! I thought he was in England. What happened?'

197

'He lost the job.'

'What will he do now?'

Stefania shrugs. 'I try not to care, but it's difficult.'

Pia goes with her to the door. Outside in the street, on the corner of the piazza, Taj is sitting on a small stool in his red robes with the woven hat covered in bells, and he is honking into his long Alpenhorn, wailing up at the balloon moon floating above him. He has moved from his pitch outside the Bank of Rapallo because the bank has closed – one day it was there, the next morning the doors were locked and men were taking down the sign from the wall.

Pia watches Stefania pause to put a coin in Taj's bowl. The Alpenhorn makes a melancholy sound, echoing down the narrow street, and Pia can't account for the spontaneous surge of joy that bubbles up inside her for no reason at all. Behind her she can hear the chatter of guests and the clink of glasses. One of the girls is singing a few notes of the Santa Lucia hymn and someone is laughing. Mari-Elena comes to stand in the doorway beside Pia and together they look out towards the piazza, where Matteo is lighting the candles in big glass jars, where in a moment everyone will walk up towards the bar to continue the party. Mari-Elena strokes the baby's head and then puts her arm around Pia's shoulders.

Pia suddenly has a desire to say something, to put into words this feeling that she has for Matteo, for this life, for the kindness of strangers, for the child who is looking at her so solemnly. But she cannot, in Greek, in Italian, or in English, find the right words.

Glossary of Italian Words and Phrases

amico/ amica – friend

artigiano, plural *artigiani* - artisan/s (literally)
   - skilled technicians in the marble studios.

auguri tutti - season's greetings everyone

Avvocato – lawyer

badante – a carer

Basta! – that's enough, stop.

Bellissima! – a very beautiful girl

Briscola – a popular card game played in the bars

buon anno - happy new year

caffè corretto – an espresso 'corrected'
   with a shot of grappa or sambuca

canile – kennel, animal rescue centre

capo d'anno - the new year (lit: 'the head of the year')

caro/ cara - darling

ci vediamo, ci rivediamo – we'll see each other (again soon)

come state? - how are you (pl)

come va? - how is it going? (formal)

comune – the local council

denuncia – an accusation, or
   'denouncement' to the authorities

Dio abbia pietà di noi - God have mercy on us

edicola – a kiosk selling newspapers and magazines

fine d'anno - the end of the year

ghiri – large dormice that live in the trees, have
   fluffy tails like squirrels and hibernate in winter

Giu! Subito! – down here immediately

Il gran caldo - the big heat

Il povero topolino - the poor little mouse

In bocca al lupo – good luck! (lit: 'in the mouth of the wolf')

in pensione - to be a pensioner

la crisi – the banking crisis that
   precipitated a Europe-wide recession

Passeggiata - the evening stroll in the piazza

pazzo - mad, crazy

piccionaia – pigeon house

molto simpatica - a very nice woman

non simpatico - not a nice man

nulla - nothing

Omaggio di Michelangelo – a homage to Michelangelo

poliziotto/ polizziotti - policeman/men

porca misere - miserable pig - a popular Italian expletive

porca puttana - pig of a prostitute, a much stronger expletive

porca dio – pig of a god - a very strong expletive

ruolotte – caravans

la sala – the hallway

Sindaco - mayor

speriamo – we hope so

straniero/ straniera/ stranieri – stranger/s, foreigner/s

sul serio - properly serious

terremoto – earthquake, tremor

una carta - a credit card

una donna forte – a strong woman

un casino - a mess

va bene - it goes well,

vaffanculo - strong expletive, equivalent of 'fuck off'

Vernacoliere - a satirical magazine - the Italian
  equivalent of Private Eye, but much ruder!

Other Books By Kathleen Jones

Biography
Catherine Cookson: Child of the Tyne, The Book Mill
Norman Nicholson: The Whispering Poet, The Book Mill
Margaret Forster: A Life in Books, The Book Mill
Katherine Mansfield: The Storyteller, Penguin NZ,
         Edinburgh University Press
Seeking Catherine Cookson's Da, Constable Robinson
Catherine Cookson: The Biography, Times Warner
A Passionate Sisterhood: The Sisters, Wives and Daughters
         of the Lake Poets, Virago & The Book Mill
Christina Rossetti: Learning Not To Be First,   Oxford
         University Press & The Book Mill,
Margaret Cavendish: A Glorious Fame,: The Life of the Duchess
         of Newcastle, Bloomsbury & The Book Mill

Fiction
Three and Other Stories, The Book Mill
The Sun's Companion, The Book Mill
The Centauress, The Book Mill

Travel
Travelling to the Edge of the World, The Book Mill

Poetry
The Rainmaker's Wife, Indigo Dreams Publishing
Mapping Emily, Templar Poetry
Not Saying Goodbye at Gate 21, Templar Poetry
Unwritten Lives, Redbeck Press

<u>Anthology</u>
Other People's Lives, The Book Mill

Non Fiction

<u>As Kate Gordon</u>
Published by Constable Robinson

An Alternative Guide to Weddings
An Alternative Guide to Baptism and Baby-naming
An Alternative Guide to Funerals

What Readers say about Kathleen Jones' Work

'A compelling narrative of a writer's passion for her work'
  Helen Dunmore, [Katherine Mansfield: The Storyteller]

'What a wonderful story it is.'
  Margaret Forster [A Passionate Sisterhood]

' *. . reading it becomes a gripping, almost addictive experience.'*
  Angela Leighton, TLS, [A Passionate Sisterhood]

'I read it with huge enjoyment - I think it's by far
the best biography yet.'
  Dame Jacqueline Wilson,
  [Katherine Mansfield: The Storyteller]

'I found the Sun's Companion an engrossing read, hard
to put down. If you like to "disappear" into the world
of a book you'll find this a satisfying read.'
  Linda Gillard, author of 'Cauldstane' and 'House
  of Silence'

'*Kathleen Jones (no relation) is such a good writer and never more so than when she is writing about people engaged in the creative process - sculptors and painters as well as writers.*'
Julia Jones [Three and Other Stories]

'*Utterly gripping and I didn't want it to end.*'
Debbie Bennett [The Sun's Companion]

'*A perceptive, beautiful, and ultimately inspirational novel.*'
Mari Biella [The Centauress]

'*This is such a bravura exercise in biography, I would suggest Kathleen Jones not only wins her case but should be awarded costs.*'
Charlotte Cory, TLS,
[Catherine Cookson: The Biography]